HER STAND-IN BOYFRIEND

KELLY JAMIESON

Entangled Publishing, LLC
2614 South Timberline Road
Suite 109
Fort Collins, CO 80525
Visit our website at www.entangledpublishing.com.

Select is an imprint of Entangled Publishing, LLC.

Edited by Karen Grove and Jessica Snyder
Cover design by Nat Anderson from Kanaxa Designs
Cover art from iStock

Manufactured in the United States of America

First Edition July 2015

To my husband, as always, for supporting me through all this craziness.

Chapter One

How much worse could things get?

This never happened at events Lexi organized. Sure, there were problems from time to time. She couldn't control *everything*, much as she tried with her checklists, notes, and backup plans. Over the years, she'd learned to stay calm when problems arose, because no matter what, she would figure out a solution and make things at least *appear* perfect to her clients and their guests. She swore they would never know about any snafus or screwups.

Sadly, there was no way to hide the problems tonight and make things appear perfect.

With her insides in knots, Lexi attempted to console a sobbing Mrs. Jacobs while Mr. Jacobs tossed back yet another glass of Laguvulin. "The guests are all eating," she told Mrs. Jacobs, standing in the hall outside the Grande Salon at the swank Cavanaugh Club. "They seem to be enjoying the meal."

Mr. Jacobs snorted. Lexi bugged her eyes out at him, and he grimaced, then patted his wife's shoulder. "Sheesh right," he slurred. "It's just food."

"It's not just food!" Mrs. Jacobs wailed. "This dinner was supposed to be sophisticated and elegant!" She sobbed again.

The Jacobs were a well-known power couple in Chicago, and Steve Jacobs had planned this big bash for his wife Liza's fortieth birthday. Lexi had been thrilled to work with such prominent clients, knowing this could lead to more great jobs for her events planning company, Papillon.

She fought to keep her expression calm, her heart giving a squeeze of sympathy for the other woman. Lexi felt her pain—she, too, had wanted this event to be perfect. Her insides went hollow thinking about how bad this could be for her reputation. "Let's go into the ladies' room and fix your makeup," she said in a gentle voice. "Then you can go back in there and finish your dinner."

"I'm not even hungry anymore." Mrs. Jacobs sniffled, but let Lexi lead her to the bathroom.

Luckily Lexi carried a "tool kit" to every event she planned, which contained scissors, pliers, tape, wire, elastics, push pins, safety pins, and a whole lot more, but also a tube of mascara, concealer, and powder. This wasn't the kind of emergency she'd expected when she'd included those items. A sobbing, distraught client was not something she ever wanted to deal with. Or had ever had to deal with in the past.

"There are a lot of lovely gifts out there," she said, trying to get Mrs. Jacobs's mind off the dinner. "I'm sure you're looking forward to opening them."

Finally they returned to the party. People were eating,

although Lexi had caught the surprised looks and exchanged glances as plates had been served. She sighed.

She'd recently started using a new caterer for parties, and they'd seemed awesome...until they'd disappeared off the face of Chicago. Yesterday, she'd spent the day making frantic phone calls trying to find someone who could cater the party for a hundred guests at such short notice. She'd ended up with Baba Yaworski's Ukrainian Catering. Sadly the cabbage rolls, pierogis, and kielbasa were not what Mr. and Mrs. Jacobs had in mind for their elegant party.

On top of the meal problem, the pretty birthday cake Lexi had ordered from the same caterer was also a no-show. It was going to be beautiful, a huge black and white polka-dotted cake topped with a big pink fondant bow. Thankfully, Lexi's friend Jamie, a pastry chef just starting her own business, had saved the day by whipping up several cakes for her that morning. They were nothing like the amazing creation she'd originally planned, but at least it was cake. Unfortunately, those cakes had also made Liza Jacobs cry since they weren't the beautiful cake she'd expected.

Mrs. Jacobs sat next to her husband, who had refilled his glass of scotch for about the hundredth time that night. As Lexi turned away, a man in a dark suit approached her.

"You're the event planner?" he asked.

"Yes. Lexi Mannis." She extended her hand to shake his.

"I'm the head of security," he said. "We're going to move the gifts to a more secure location."

"I'm sure they're fine here," she said. "But okay." She needed to get the cake with the candle ready to bring out.

After a big production of guests singing along to "Happy Birthday" played over the sound system, a still-miserable

Mrs. Jacobs blew out the single sparkler. A swarm of servers descended to cut and serve the cakes. Luckily, they were delicious—red velvet with cream cheese frosting. Her friend Mac's favorite. Maybe she could scrounge a piece to take home, since he was coming over tomorrow.

Lexi's nerves started to settle. As the time neared for Mrs. Jacobs to open her gifts, she went in search of the security guy who'd moved them.

But nobody at the club knew who she was talking about.

"We don't have security staff," the assistant manager told her.

Their eyes met, and Lexi's insides seized again as fear turned her blood to ice water. Staff members helped her look, but the gifts were nowhere to be found.

Pressure built behind her cheekbones, and she fought back tears. This could not be happening.

"There has to be some mistake," she said to the assistant manager. "Please tell me someone didn't just steal all the gifts."

He frowned, looking as ill as she felt. "It kinda looks that way."

"Oh shit." Shit shit shit. How was she going to tell Mrs. Jacobs about this?

She resisted the urge to make a run for it. That would be much easier. But she couldn't do that, or she'd never get another job again.

Although, that might happen anyway after this epic disaster.

They had to call the police, of course, which totally put a damper on the rest of the evening. Guests started leaving, muttering to themselves, while Mrs. Jacobs locked herself in a bathroom stall, crying again.

By the time she was ready to go home, Lexi's head was pounding. She'd dealt with the police and the staff at the club, and attempted to soothe Mrs. Jacobs. There wasn't anything more she could do.

In the cloakroom, she set down her purse, her tool kit, and the small box with the piece of red velvet cake in it for Mac, then tugged her coat from a hanger. She wearily slipped her arms into it, eager to get home and forget about the disastrous evening. Lifting her hair from beneath the collar, she turned to see Mr. Jacobs swaying on his feet and eyeing her with a look that made a shiver crawl down her spine. She forced a smile. "I'm sorry again, Mr. Jacobs."

He moved closer, and she stepped back. And stepped back again. "This party was a disashter," he said. Then he reached for her.

Her heart leaped into her throat, and her eyes flew open wide. She smacked his hands away, stumbling back, but she hit the wall. "What are you doing?"

"I'll still pay your bill," he said. "If you do what I want. Right now."

"What? What do you want?" Adrenaline surged through her veins, making her knees wobble and her hands shake.

"You." He leaned in and tried to kiss her.

Ack! She turned her head and dodged his mouth, smelling the booze on his breath. Her stomach rolled and her heart thudded. Forget about getting paid! Trapped between him and the wall, she gave him another shove, but despite being completely shellacked on Scotch, he didn't move. "No! Get away from me!"

He still tried to kiss her, his hands now on her body.

Shit.

She did the only thing she could think of. She lifted her knee in a sharp move that connected with his junk.

"Argh!" He stumbled back and bent at the waist, clutching his crotch. "What the fuck?"

Lexi looked up to see Mrs. Jacobs standing in the door of the cloakroom, her red eyes big as plates. "What is going on?" she demanded.

Lexi closed her own eyes briefly.

Yep, her event planning business was toast.

Burned toast.

She grabbed her things and walked out of the club onto West Superior Street, tapping down the dark sidewalk in her high heels. She'd been on her feet all night, and her soles burned. As did her stomach. And her eyes.

Wow. Things had been going incredibly well for her business, and now all the work she had put into building her reputation was crumbling.

Lexi entered the parking garage and found her car where she'd parked it earlier, tossing her tool kit into the trunk before climbing into the driver's seat. She set her purse and the piece of birthday cake on the passenger seat. For a moment she gripped the steering wheel, shaking her head. Letting out another sigh, she put the car in reverse and backed out of the parking spot.

Grateful to be back home in the little apartment she shared with her best friend Vanda, she finally kicked off the stiletto pumps. Vanda was out, and the apartment was dark and quiet. Lexi padded in bare feet to the kitchen in search of the bottle of wine they'd opened last night. She frowned, peering into the fridge. Gone. No wine. Son of a bucket.

She heaved a sigh and turned to go to her room. Nibbling her bottom lip, she eyed the box with the red velvet cake where she'd set it on the counter. *No.* That was for Mac. Her secret stash of gummy bears would have to suffice tonight.

She frowned as she squeezed past the big cardboard boxes taking up space in the hall. Her new IKEA dresser and nightstand had been sitting there for almost a week. Mac was coming tomorrow to help build them. Thank god, because she was totally inept when it came to stuff like that.

As she chewed gummy bears and got ready for bed, she tried not to replay every pathetic detail of the evening in her mind, but it was hard not to. She loved her job, and her business was important to her. How could absolutely everything go wrong at the same time?

After she'd graduated from college with a business degree, she'd worked in the corporate world for a while, but then took a year off to travel. She'd figured she'd come back and find another job easily enough, but that didn't happen. However, she'd also discovered that the corporate world of finance wasn't as much fun as she'd thought it would be, as in, it was no fun at all. She'd decided to try to make a living doing something that *was* fun…something she'd always enjoyed, which was planning parties.

With the professional relationships she had cultivated through her previous job, the connections she had via her two dads, and even the networking opportunities her friendship with Mac provided, her business had taken off. The name of the business, Papillon, came from the fact that in college she was known as a social butterfly. It had been almost two years since she'd started Papillon, and things had been going great.

Until tonight. Now her reputation was probably trashed. All the people at the party would talk about it, and who would hire her knowing about that disaster? And what if the Jacobs decided not to pay their bill?

Sleep eluded her as she lay in her bed with her stomach in knots, awake for a good part of the night.

• • •

Mac sat on the floor in Lexi's living room Sunday afternoon with pieces of furniture spread out around him.

"You need to read the directions," Lexi said, sitting cross-legged on the couch.

"No I don't." He totally knew what he was doing. Thank Christ, because Lex was useless. Gorgeous. Smart, absolutely. But not when it came to building furniture.

"How did the party go last night?" He peered at a dark square of laminated fiberboard.

"Oh my god. Don't even ask." She fell back into the couch cushions, closing her eyes.

"What?" He frowned.

"It was a total nightmare. You know how I couldn't get hold of the caterer?"

"Yeah." She'd mentioned it last weekend when they'd bought the IKEA furniture, which was too heavy for her to carry alone. He'd figured she'd reach them eventually.

"Well, I never did find them. They've apparently gone out of business or something, and I had to find someone else last minute."

He set down the Allen wrench and gave her his full attention. Her red-gold hair tumbled in waves around her shoulders, and even dressed in a baggy sweater and leggings, she looked sweet and sexy. He watched a host of emotions scroll across her face as she talked, her green eyes getting shiny, her pretty mouth trembling. When her voice quivered, his chest clenched. *Fuck, she's really upset about this.*

"And then he grabbed me and tried to kiss me."

Mac's body jolted, and his forehead tightened. "What the fuck?"

"Apparently he would overlook everything and still pay me if I let him nail me in the cloakroom."

"Jesus fucking Christ." Mac leaped to his feet and strode three steps to the couch. He dropped down beside her. "Are you okay?"

"I'm fine." She sighed. "I kneed him in the nuts."

Mac choked. "Oh."

"Right in front of his wife. Happy birthday to her."

"Fuck, Lex… He touched you?" Rage rose inside him in a scorching blast. "Who is this asshole? I'm gonna—"

"No, you're not." She touched her fingers to his lips. "I'm fine. He was so drunk he probably would've had whisky dick anyway."

"What the hell do you know about whisky dick? Never mind." He closed his mind off to the idea of Lexi and another guy's dick.

"It's done. It was an epic disaster, but it's done." She sighed. "And possibly so is my business."

"Bullshit. Your business will be fine." He reached out and pulled her in for a hug.

Probably a mistake, because his body responded to the feel of her soft curves against him with a familiar stirring down south. But damn, she was upset, and he wanted to make her feel better.

"It'll be fine," he murmured, his cheek against her hair. "It was only one party. None of it was your fault."

"Of course it was. I'm the event planner. It's up to me to make sure everything goes perfectly."

"You didn't know someone was going to steal the gifts… *And* the caterer would go out of business… *And* your client was a drunken lech… But, heck, you said the cake was good."

She huffed out a laugh. "Thank you, Mac. I can always count on you to put things in perspective."

He grinned and gave her a squeeze. "Your business is a success because you're good at what you do. You know it. I know it. And so do all of your clients."

She shrugged.

"I've told you before, you need to sell yourself better. Don't be modest. You *are* good at it. You love planning and making lists. With your business background and the cool ideas you come up with, plus the fact that you're so anal—er, I mean, detail oriented—of course your business is a success. And it will continue to be."

"I shouldn't have let that guy take the gifts."

"You had no idea he was a thief." He squeezed her again. "Come on. Don't beat yourself up over things you couldn't control."

She pulled back and gave him a watery smile. "Thank you." The warm softness in her eyes had his gut twisting. "Okay. You made me feel better. Now. Back to my furniture."

Jesus. The idea of some fuckwit groping her made his stomach churn and his fists clench. How was he supposed to forget that and build a fucking dresser? He sucked in a long breath through his nose and then exhaled. "Right." He moved off the couch, his blood still running hot. She was okay. Well, she'd hurt the guy, so there was that.

He lowered himself back to the floor to resume the construction project.

Moments later, Lexi said, "That's such a tiny little tool."

"That's not what my last girlfriend said." He looked up and met her eyes, and damn, he loved the smile and the choked laugh she gave. He grinned back at her.

They were friends.

Right.

When he'd met Lexi in college six years ago, he'd been dating someone else, but it hadn't been long before he was so crazy for Lexi that he'd broken up with Brittany. Because he'd been off limits when they met, Lexi saw him as a friend and that was it. She'd dated other guys—hell, guys had been lined up at her door. Her red hair and freckles should have given her a Raggedy Ann look, should have been more of a turn-off than a turn-on. But her energy, smart mouth, and frequent laughter drew people in. As he'd gotten to know her better, she'd become more and more attractive…her pretty face, bright eyes and sweet smile, and an ass that could make him hard with just a glimpse of it in a pair of snug jeans.

He looked down at the Allen wrench in his hand and tried to refocus. He searched the floor for what he needed.

"What are you looking for?" Lexi asked.

"I need a screw."

"You and me both," she muttered.

Oh, hell no. He could not let his thoughts wander down that torturous path. Instead he forced a laugh. "Hey, speak for yourself."

She giggled, and again he was glad he'd made her laugh.

She wanted sex? Interesting. She hadn't dated anyone in a while. She said it was because she was too busy and boyfriends were too much work.

"When you're done, I have a reward for you," she said.

No. Don't even go there, asshole.

He squeezed his eyes closed, the guy downstairs once again stirring in his jeans.

Down, boy.

He cleared his throat. "Oh, yeah? What's that?"

"Red velvet cake."

He glanced up.

She nodded, her eyes alight. "With cream cheese icing. I saved a piece from last night. You can have it after the dinner I promised I'd cook you for helping."

"Okay. There's some motivation to get this done."

It wasn't sex with Lexi, but hey, since that was never going to happen, red velvet cake was the next best thing. Well, not really. But it was the best he was going to get.

Chapter Two

"An art gallery opening? Seriously, Lex?" Mac groaned on the other end of the phone ten days later.

"Seriously. Come on, Mac. This event could lead to some new business, and I don't want to go alone."

"Take one of your girls."

"None of my friends can come. Vanda's going home to her parents for the weekend, Mia has some family thing, and Kaylee has a date. Don't make me go alone."

She sensed he was softening.

"This is a big event. There'll be a lot of potential clients there. You know I need the business."

His sigh drifted through the phone, which meant he knew she was right and he was giving in. Maybe. She hoped.

"You have a job coming up," he pointed out. "For me."

"True." He'd hired her to plan a business function his company was holding to celebrate the completion of a big project with one of their major clients. "But that's one job."

She grimaced, squeezing her eyes closed briefly. "The Jacobs ended up paying only half what they owed me, which was fair considering the disaster. At first, they were refusing to pay anything, but I had to cover all *my* costs. I need more work, and I need it soon. After what happened that night, if word gets around, I'll be lucky if I ever land another job in my life." Her stomach dropped to her toes thinking back to that day.

"Don't be dramatic."

Her lips twitched into a reluctant smile. He knew her too well.

"I know it wasn't the most successful party," he said, "but you *will* get more business."

"One client canceled right after, when they heard the story, and I've had no calls about new events. Probably because of that story in the paper about the gifts being stolen. What does that tell you?"

"It tells me you're in a slow period. A normal business cycle."

"Yeah, right." She sighed. "At this point, I'd even take a job planning a wedding."

He laughed. "Christ, that's serious."

It was. She had no desire to be a wedding planner. Weddings were huge and stressful, and dealing with bridezillas definitely took the fun out of party planning. She generally turned down requests to plan weddings, but she'd do almost anything else, from birthdays and anniversaries and bar and bat mitzvahs, to corporate functions like Christmas parties and staff appreciation events.

"Whatever," she said. "I need business. I *need* to go to this party."

"What kind of art are they showing?" he asked. "Is it like that gallery you dragged me to where the paintings were all abstract shit that were supposedly symbols of cosmic visions and ethereal nights where dreams exist in a raw state untouched by rational thought?"

She burst out laughing. "No! Hahaha. This might even be kind of interesting. It's all black and white photographs celebrating Chicago architecture. Very relatable."

"Fuck. Whatever. All right. Do I have to wear a suit?"

Amused, she plucked a dead leaf off the African violet plant sitting on the windowsill in her apartment and moved to drop it in a wastebasket near the desk. "You wear suits all the time now."

"And still hate it."

"I think this *is* a suit and tie kind of deal," she said regretfully.

"Suit," he clipped. "No tie. Take it or leave it."

"Deal."

"What time?"

"Pick me up at seven."

"You the designated driver? Otherwise we're cabbing it. I am not going to a gallery opening without consuming large quantities of alcohol."

"What if I told you it was a dry event?"

"You're shitting me."

"Yeah." She laughed. "I am. There *will* be booze."

"Thank Christ."

"We can take a cab." She also wanted to have a few drinks, if not large quantities of alcohol as Mac planned. With some guys, she'd be worried they were going to get drunk and embarrass her in front of potential clients, but not Mac. She could count on him. That's why he was such a perfect stand-in boyfriend.

"Okay. Fine. See you Friday night."

"Mac?"

"Yeah?"

"Thank you." Gratitude softened her voice. She truly did appreciate him coming to this event with her.

"You owe me," he growled and ended the call. She just smiled as she tapped her cell phone screen.

She turned to Vanda, who sat on the couch, feet perched on the coffee table, pink foam separators spreading her toes as she applied indigo polish to each nail.

"He's gonna do it, isn't he?" Vanda didn't look up from her pedicure.

"Yeah."

She shook her head. "I don't know how you do that, Lexi."

"Do what?"

"Macauley Northrop is a multi-millionaire tech entrepreneur with all kinds of women after him. He's arrogant and aloof and unfriendly. But you call him up and within a couple of minutes have him convinced to go to some artsy gallery opening that he wouldn't normally be caught dead at."

"He's not unfriendly," Lexi said slowly, moving to sit on the chair adjacent to the sofa. "We're friends."

"I guess." Vanda shook her head. "He seems to come running every time you snap your fingers. Sounds like more than friendship."

Lexi frowned. "That's ridiculous. I mean, we *could* be more than friends. We get along great. We have since college.

But why ruin a great friendship? We're both on the same page there. And it's perfect having him to fall back on when I need a date at times like this."

This wasn't the first time she'd called on Mac to go somewhere with her. Not that she didn't have dates. She dated. Sort of. She met guys, they hooked up, saw each other a few times, then they got annoyed that she worked long hours and was focused on building her business, and they disappeared. Most guys needed too much time and attention. The only guy who'd stuck around for any length of time was Hector, and they'd broken up months ago. She'd been disappointed but, honestly, not heartbroken. She didn't have time for a boyfriend *and* her business *and* yoga classes *and* staying in touch with her girlfriends, too.

Her lack of a boyfriend was inconvenient when she wanted to go somewhere and didn't have a date, not to mention when she needed her new IKEA furniture built, but that was where Mac came in. It worked perfectly for both of them. He was good with an Allen wrench, and she repaid him with red velvet cake and chicken parmigiana. And beer. Last weekend they'd gone to the Craft Beer Festival, something they both wanted to do. Lexi's girlfriends weren't interested, but Mac liked beer and food, as did she, so they'd gone and had a great time. They also both liked hockey, which none of her girlfriends did, and he often invited her to Blackhawks games. She got to sit in his private suite and partake of his generous booze and food.

Hmm. It seemed many of their interactions involved booze and food. Something they both enjoyed.

But it wasn't all one-sided. Mac made out on this arrangement, too. He often had clients at games, and she schmoozed with them, which helped him out, kind of like having a hostess. Truthfully, it helped her, too, because the rich businessmen he hung out with had more than once turned into clients for her business.

"What are you going to wear?" Vanda screwed the cap back on her bottle of polish.

Right. The gallery opening. A chance to salvage her career. "Good question!" This made her sit up and think. "One of my little black dresses, I guess."

"Ugh."

"What? What's wrong with my little black dresses?"

"You wear those all the time when you're working. You need something new. Something...pink."

Lexi blinked. "Pink?"

"Or red. I don't know. Just something not black."

Lexi frowned. "I like black."

"I know." Vanda rolled her eyes. "Look at you."

Lexi looked down at her black, long-sleeved T-shirt and black pants. Fashionable, yes, the shirt snug, the pants low rise with a narrow belt and wide leg. But definitely black. She wore black dresses on purpose when she was working an event so as to blend into the background as she did her stuff.

"We should go shopping," Vanda said.

"I can't afford to go shopping. I have no work, remember?"

"That's what credit cards are for."

Lexi made a face. "Right."

"I'll rally the troops." Vanda studied her polished toes. "We'll do dinner and then shop for a new dress for you. Maybe shoes, too."

"I have shoes."

"You have *black* shoes. If you buy a red dress you'll

need…um…nude shoes. Maybe ivory."

"Oh my god, I can't afford shoes, too!"

"Sure you can."

"I have some savings, but being self-employed is scary. I can't go crazy."

"Stop being sensible," Vanda complained, then sighed. "I can hear my credit cards squealing in fear in my wallet as we speak."

"And there is no way in H E double hockey sticks that I am wearing pink. Have you ever seen me wear pink?"

"No."

"There's a reason for that. I look hideous in pink." Her red hair, on the light side of auburn but not as light as strawberry blond, and fair skin, with a tendency to freckle in the summer, did not go well with pink. "Also, red is a problem if it's too close to pink."

"Purple."

She winced. "Not sure about that."

"Peach. Maybe a pinky peach."

Lexi was done with this conversation. "Want some popcorn?"

"Ooooh, yeah."

• • •

Mac texted with Lexi a couple of times during the week, then Friday afternoon he picked up his phone to call her. A gallery opening was the last thing he wanted to go to, but on the other hand, it was Lexi.

Sitting in his office in the Trent Building, looking out over the downtown Chicago skyline, his jaw clenched. Why did he keep doing this to himself?

She was never going to see him as more than her geeky friend from college. She kept asking him out but was always very clear that they were just friends. Sometimes, admittedly, *he* did the asking, because try as he might, he couldn't end things with her. Even though every fucking time he saw her, his heart cracked a little more. Each time they were together, he wanted to touch her, kiss her, strip her naked and... well...no point going there.

He'd been in this miserable mix of heaven and hell for six long years.

He tapped his phone to call her number. "Hey, Lex. Still on for tonight?"

"Yes, we're still on. Don't sound so hopeful that we're not."

He rubbed his fingertips over the tightness between his eyebrows. "Been a long week. There better be good beverages there."

"I'm sure there will be."

He ended the call. Was he a complete idiot? Maybe the biggest thing that kept him from ending this torturous relationship was the thought that if he didn't go with her to these things, she'd ask someone else.

All through college, and even after, she'd dated other guys. Every time she'd started seeing someone, it was like a knife stabbing into his gut. Watching her flirt and hold hands and kiss guys, seeing her sit on their laps at parties and make out had made him nuts. He'd dealt with it by dating other girls, telling himself he'd find someone else, which had never been fair to the other girls because it was never going to happen, as he'd come to realize.

Maybe it would happen if he stayed the hell away from Lexi. But she wanted to be friends, and he was weak when it came to her, as helpless as an addict who needed a fix.

He didn't bother going home to change after work since she'd insisted on him wearing a suit. The car service he used dropped him off at her apartment, and he asked the driver to wait.

Lexi opened the door, and he took one look at her in some sparkly, shimmery ivory dress that hugged every curve, swallowed, and said, "Hey. Got any beer?"

"Pre-gaming?" She moved to the fridge.

He followed behind her, his gaze tracking from her bright coppery hair down over that hot little body and long, sleek legs. "Got a problem with that?"

"Not at all." She opened the fridge door and bent over. Christ. Her dress stretched over her ass, cupping it and displaying it most excellently. His dick instantly hardened, as usual. Then she rose and turned, and damn, he had to jerk his gaze away from her ass fast. Shit. She'd noticed him ogling her.

But as usual, for her it was no big deal. She grinned. "Like my dress?" She walked toward him in bare feet and handed him the beer.

"It's very...sparkly." He took the beer, twisted off the cap, and lifted it to his lips, guzzling with near desperate haste. "You look like a Christmas ornament."

She gave a shocked gasp. "What? A Christmas ornament?" She looked down at herself.

Hell. He did this all the time. He wanted to tell her that she was so fucking gorgeous she blew his fucking mind. Instead, what came out was an insult. He forced a grin, used to this game. "Kidding. It's nice."

"Nice? Huh." Her smile went crooked. "Two hundred dollars worth of nice. And that was on sale. But thanks."

It was a simple dress—round neckline, cap sleeves, ivory color. It was the way it fit that made it sexy, hugging her body all the way down to right above the knees. Swirls of sequins and beaded ribbons, all in clear or ivory, made her shimmer.

"I guess I have time for a drink, too," she said.

"Sure." Mac wandered over to sit on her couch. "Car service is waiting downstairs."

"I thought you said we'd take a taxi."

"Car service. Taxi. Whatever."

She smiled and shook her head at him. She liked to bug Mac about his money. To him it was no big deal.

With a glass of wine in hand, she sat beside him on the couch. The snug dress rode up a little on smooth thighs, attracting his attention yet again. And again, he dragged his gaze off her gorgeous legs.

"I can't eat anything tonight," she remarked.

He lifted an eyebrow. "Why not?"

"Well, A, the dress is tight."

"I hadn't noticed," he murmured.

"And B, it's ivory. You know what I'm like."

"True. White wine it is."

Lexi had an entirely deserved reputation for spilling things on herself. And on anyone standing near enough to be in the danger zone. He and her other friends liked to tease her and exaggerate it, but she totally made fun of herself, too.

"You look nice." Her gaze skimmed over his charcoal suit. He'd lost the tie after his last meeting of the day, and his dark shirt was now open at the collar.

"Thanks," he said dryly. She could do understatement as well as he could. Except she was being real, and he was desperately trying to keep his tongue from hanging out of his mouth.

"Why did you have such a bad week?"

"Lots of shit going on." His shoulders tensed briefly, and he looked at his beer.

"Tell me."

"Well, for one thing, Justin quit." Justin Karp was one his best developers.

She blinked. "Whoa. Why?"

Mac shrugged and leaned back. "Better offer somewhere else." He knew his voice held an edge. He and his business partners took pride in keeping their staff long term, which wasn't the norm in the tech biz where people bounced around like pinballs, sometimes ending back at the same company multiple times. "Wish he'd talked to us before he took the job."

"Yeah. Shit. What are you going to do? Promote someone else? Recruit from outside?"

"Not sure yet. Pete and I spent half the day talking about it and looking at who we already have working for us. We have lots of talented people."

"Yeah. You do. And you guys have a great reputation."

He shrugged. Lately there'd been a bunch of blog articles written about him and the company, sometimes with other successful young entrepreneurs under thirty years old. When he'd first graduated from college he'd worked for a big web developer for a while, then started his own business. Centric was an online media company and information provider that created content for web professionals — developers, designers, programmers, freelancers, and website owners. Since then, his business had spun off several others — a graphic design studio, a firm that bought and sold websites, and a company that developed web and mobile applications. Now they had people knocking on their door looking for opportunities to work with them.

"But you have HR people now, right?" she continued. "They'll help with hiring."

"Yeah. But you know I'll need to be involved."

She smiled as her lips touched the rim of her wine glass. "Really? I can't believe that."

He turned his head and gave her a narrow-eyed look, but they both ended up laughing.

"Guess we better head out," he said, lifting the beer to peer at it to judge how much was left. Then he drained it. "Are you *sure* we have to go to this?"

She pouted, but he recognized it as fake. "Yes! This is business for me, trying to find new clients — remember?"

His lips twitched. "I remember. Okay. Let's go. Thanks for the brew."

"Any time, dude. Let me find my shoes and my purse."

"Where's Vanda tonight?" he called as she disappeared down the hall to her bedroom. The apartment was small enough that you could practically have a conversation with someone from any room.

"She's gone home for the weekend," Lexi yelled back. "It's her mom's birthday."

"Oh, yeah." The reason Vanda couldn't have gone with Lex tonight.

A moment later she returned, now wearing a sexy pair

of ivory shoes that matched the dress and carrying a tiny purse.

"Oh wait! I forgot business cards. Doh." She snapped back down the hall in the spiky heels, her ass twitching in the form-fitting dress.

He leaned against the kitchen counter waiting for her. When she returned, he couldn't help but give her another look up and down, this time his gaze lingering on the shoes. He lifted an eyebrow. "You could take out a snake's eye with those shoes."

She laughed but shook her head. "You couldn't just give me a compliment? You have to be a smartass?"

He grinned and pushed away from the counter, then hooked his arm around her neck. Damn, she smelled good, too, the light lemony-grapefruit scent he would forever know as hers. That almost undid him, but he held onto casual by a thread. "Let's go, babe."

Chapter Three

The Sloan Gallery was right on Michigan Avenue, at street level of a sleek, modern high-rise. Lexi had to admit it was cool not to have to worry about parking or cab fare. Mac used a car service regularly, and she guessed he paid some kind of monthly fee or something. The driver opened her door, and she emerged onto the wide sidewalk in the brisk spring evening. It wasn't yet dark and the sidewalks still teemed with pedestrians, traffic crowding Michigan Avenue as always.

She'd moved to Chicago with her dads when she was sixteen, stayed to go to college, and although she'd left for a year to travel Europe, she never wanted to live anywhere else. The architecture, the old buildings mixed with the ultra-modern, the nightlife, the food, and all the different neighborhoods made it a special city. With the immense blue stretch of Lake Michigan, it felt almost like living on the ocean. She'd lived there eight years and still hadn't seen everything there was to see.

Mac took her arm to lead her into the gallery—such a gentleman. Vanda wasn't sure if she liked him, because he wasn't very talkative. Sometimes he came across as unfriendly, but Lexi knew he was protective and courteous, and...well...reserved might be a good word.

He could certainly be aggressive in the business world, and he could definitely charm investors and clients when he had to. But she'd known him for six years and knew he was happiest in small groups, talking geek stuff and drinking beer, or playing around on his computer.

She stopped outside the door and held him back.

He looked down at her. He was six foot two and she was only five foot four—although her three-inch heels helped. "What?"

"I just want to say thank you again for coming." She smiled, but this was in all seriousness. "I know this isn't your thing. I really do appreciate it."

His eyes softened and warmed, and the corners of his mouth lifted. "Any time, Lex."

They smiled at each other, and her heart gave a funny flutter. Then he pulled the door open for her to enter the gallery.

Shiny light hardwood floors stretched out in front of them, and lights on tracks above illuminated the photographs hanging on white walls. Already, the place was full of people. They checked their coats, then Lexi presented her invitation to a girl sitting at a table who handed them materials on the exhibit.

Servers with trays of appetizers mingled through the crowd.

"Let's find the bar." Mac set his hand on the small of her back to lead her across the room. "I'm gonna need a drink to get through this."

They easily located the bar by the crowd of people surrounding it and made their way there to wait in a line. She went on tiptoes to ask the question into his ear. "Are you going to drink beer?" She was just bugging him. She didn't care what he drank.

He shot her a look, eyes gleaming. "Sure. Why not?"

"I get the feeling this isn't a beer-drinking crowd."

"If they serve beer, it is."

She laughed. But when he ordered Grey Goose, and a Sauvignon Blanc for her, she said, "You could have a beer if that's what you want."

"I know."

She held her glass up to clink against his. "Mr. Sophisticated."

"You think I haven't learned anything the last few years?" He smirked at her. "All those business dinners and networking functions? I may be a geek, but don't worry, I won't embarrass you."

She shook her head. "I'm not worried about that, you goof."

They meandered around, looking at the photos. She hadn't yet seen anyone she knew.

"How'd you get invited to this party anyway?" Mac asked. "Damn, I should have worn my glasses."

Lexi frowned. "Why? Aren't you wearing your contacts?"

"Yeah. I just thought the glasses would make me look more intellectual. Like that guy." He lifted his chin at a man standing across the room wearing black horn-rimmed glasses, skinny black pants, a tweed jacket, and a scarf wrapped around his neck.

She grinned. "Um, yeah." Mac may have undergone a bit of a makeover since college, but Satan would be shoveling snow before Mac ever wore skinny jeans and a scarf. The idea made her want to giggle.

"Lexi, baby."

She turned, hearing her name. "Dad!" With a big smile, she rushed into her dad's arms for a hug. "I didn't think you were going to be here! How are you?"

He beamed down at her. "Great. Glad you made it, too."

She shifted to include Mac. "You remember Mac, right, Dad?"

Mac extended a hand. "Hi, Alex."

"Mac." Dad gave him a stern look, and Mac actually winced when Dad shook his hand. "How are you?"

"Uh, good, good."

Lexi's forehead tightened as she took in Dad's expression. She thought he liked Mac. She turned to Mac and said, "I never answered your question about how I got invited tonight. This is how. Papa knows the gallery owner and some of the photographers exhibiting here."

Her other dad was a photographer who specialized in food photography, freelancing for magazines and advertising agencies, also working on gorgeous cookbooks.

"We weren't sure if we were going to be able to come," Dad said. "Had to juggle some other commitments."

"Where's Papa?" Lexi asked.

"Over there." Dad lifted his chin to his right. "Talking to one of the other photographers."

Her two dads. Yes, they were gay. They'd been together

forever, and twenty-six years ago they'd decided they wanted to be parents. Okay, make that twenty-seven years, it took a while to make a baby. Or find a baby. They'd decided on adoption and had taken her in when she was only days old, given up by a young single mom who couldn't look after her.

Papa beamed a smile at them from across the room. She smiled back and waved. He'd no doubt join them as soon as he could.

"I saw an article the other day about how online advertising spending has declined," Dad said to Mac. "Has that affected your business?"

"Sure, to some extent." Mac shrugged. "But we're still making money, and keeping our customers happy. We work hard to deliver extra value, so we haven't had to slash prices like our competitors have. And we've diversified, which has helped protect us from changes in the market."

"Diversification can spread a business too thin, though." Dad lifted one eyebrow.

Dad was a successful architect and was very active in the business world and with some high-profile charities. He was always interested in other people, but tonight, his questions sounded kind of like an interrogation. Bemused, Lexi sipped her wine, listening as Mac calmly talked about a new mobile app they'd recently brought out and how it was selling, and Dad nodded with pursed lips.

Mac was crazy smart. A feeling of pride swelled in her chest, listening to him talk. She also loved how accepting he was of her two dads. He'd just shrugged when she'd shared her family story with him, like it was no big deal. Not everyone was that open-minded, as she'd painfully learned.

When Papa joined them, she got another big hug, and

Mac another handshake.

"Nice to see you again, Mac." Papa gave him an assessing look, although he smiled as he did.

"You, too, Rob."

Papa turned to Lexi. "I need to introduce you to some people, princess. That woman I was talking to was telling me her parents' fiftieth wedding anniversary is coming up, and she wants to throw them a party."

Yes! She clasped her wine glass in both hands, bent her knees briefly, and rolled her eyes heavenward. "Great. I brought business cards."

"That's my girl." Papa nudged her shoulder, and she followed him across the room.

She loved her dads. Dad was outgoing and loved to entertain, and had a wicked sense of humor. Tall and lean, his dark hair was just starting to go a bit silver. Papa was a few inches shorter, stockier, with light brown hair, quieter than Dad—one of those "still waters run deep" kind of guys.

Papa introduced her to the woman he'd been speaking with, and Lexi handed her a card as they chatted about what kind of party she wanted.

Moments later someone touched her arm, and Lexi looked up to see a former client. One whose event had gone well. Very well. Thankfully. "Hi! How are you, Eloisa?"

"I'm great, thanks." Eloisa Meyerstein smiled at her. "Nice to see you again. People are still complimenting us on the bar mitzvah you did for us."

"Oh, thank you!" This was nice to hear in front of a prospective client, and especially after the Jacobs debacle. Lexi made introductions, and they did the small talk thing. Eloisa introduced Lexi to some friends of hers, and Lexi handed out more business cards.

Over the course of the evening, she and Mac separated at times while she met more potential clients, thanks mostly to Dad and Papa, who kept introducing her and telling people what she did. She also made mental notes of how the gallery party had been organized—the food, the drinks, the staff, the decorations. She noted things that could be done better and things she liked, and filed this all away for future reference.

As the night continued, she frequently sought out Mac, keeping an eye on where he was to make sure he was having an okay time, since he'd been good enough to come with her. He'd run into some people he knew, too. One of them was a woman who was eyeing him with a carnal gleam in her dark eyes as she talked to him. A gorgeous woman.

When Lexi and Mac had met in college, he'd been a bit geeky, with glasses and not quite cool clothes. Since he'd graduated and developed all his successful businesses, he'd gotten contact lenses, an expensive haircut, and some kind of professional wardrobe advice, because now he was hot. Vanda was not lying when she said girls were after him all the time. (Although his money also had something to do with that. No offense to Mac, but some chicks were just gold diggers.) These days he wore sexy Earnest Sewn jeans that sat low on his hips and were wrinkled and worn in strategic spots, frackin' hundred dollar Rag and Bone T-shirts, and Versace button-downs. When he had to wear a suit, like tonight, they were Armani and Prada. The fit of the suit emphasized his broad shoulders, and the dark shirt revealed his strong throat and neck. He looked better than nice—he looked hotalicious.

No wonder that chick was staring at him as if she wanted to ride him like a pony. Lexi narrowed her eyes, pressed her lips together briefly, then moved up beside Mac and slid her arm through his. "Do you need another drink, Mac?" She batted her eyelashes, peering up at him.

"Uh, sure. But I'll get it. Another wine?"

"Yes, please."

"Excuse me," Mac said to the woman before moving away. Lexi smiled at her and also stepped away.

She lost track of how many glasses of white wine she had over the evening. At one point she and Mac went to find food at the buffet. "Nice spread," he said, his gaze moving over the table. Then their eyes met, and they both burst out laughing.

Mac filled a big plate, but she only took a few little hors d'oeuvres for fear of making a mess of her dress or having to talk to someone with crumbs stuck in her lip gloss or teeth.

Things were wrapping up by ten o'clock. Lexi had a little adrenaline buzz from all the interest she'd had in her business and all the cards she'd handed out, including a couple of people who'd said they'd call and sounded serious.

"It's too early to go home," she said to Mac as they were leaving. "We're all dressed up. And you look too good to go home. Let's go somewhere else."

Something flickered in his eyes. He shook his head, but his lips twitched, and she knew she had him. "Sure." They paused out on the sidewalk, skyscrapers glittering around them. "Where do you want to go?"

"Um. How about Cobalt? It's only a few blocks from here. We can drink martinis and listen to smooth jazz."

"Okay." They slid into the town car, and Mac instructed

the driver where to take them. In the dark car, she relaxed into the seat and admired Mac—his long legs, strong shoulders, and sexy smile.

No, no, not *sexy* smile. *Nice* smile. He was a nice guy. Even if Vanda didn't think so. Peh.

The lounge was lit with ultra-cool blue and purple lighting, the perfect accent to the sultry, moody music Cobalt was known for. Sipping pomegranate martinis, she and Mac gossiped about the people they'd met at the gallery.

"That guy you introduced me to," she said. "Jack."

"Yeah? What about him?" Mac lifted an eyebrow, lounging in his tub chair. Damn, he looked good there in that dark suit, shirt open to reveal his strong throat. He held his martini glass loosely by the bowl with long fingers.

"What was his last name? I don't think I heard right."

"Kauff."

She stared at him. "I did hear right. Jack Kauff?"

"Yeah, that's right." He grinned.

"What were his parents thinking? I mean, seriously."

"Hey, I knew a guy named Mike Hunt."

She repeated it, because at first she didn't get it. Then she fell sideways in her chair, laughing. "Oh my god!"

"And of course, I went to school with Ben Dover."

She snorted, but this time she said, "Shut up! You did not."

He grinned. "Okay, maybe not. How about Dixie Rect?"

Her face started to hurt from laughing.

"Harry Ballsack?"

"Stop." She pressed a hand to her stomach, bent over the arm of her chair. "Please."

Eventually the subject turned to the design proposal her

dad was submitting for an office tower in New York City.

"If he gets it he's going to be away a lot." She pouted. "But I'm proud of him. Papa is, too. And hey, the last cookbook that Papa did is a bestseller! How about that?"

Mac reached out and covered her hand with his, rubbing with his thumb. "That's great, Lex."

She met his eyes, and his thumb stroking over her skin sent pleasant bubbles tingling through her bloodstream. Or maybe that was the martinis.

They stumbled out of the bar around one in the morning, and it was good neither of them was driving. Mac called the car service to pick them up. Back in the car, a warm buzz surrounded her.

"Hmmm," she said slowly. "I think I'm a wee bit toasted."

"Uh-oh." Mac's eyes gleamed as he smiled at her.

"Maybe I should have eaten more. On the upside, I didn't spill anything all night."

"Are you hungry?"

"Um...yeah."

So Mac had the driver go through a twenty-four-hour drive-through, and they picked up burgers, fries, and root beers, and he came up to her apartment to eat them.

"I better change out of this dress before I eat something with ketchup and mustard on it," she muttered. "Be right back."

She left him pulling the food out of the paper sack and arranging it on her coffee table, and tottered down the short hall to her room. She kicked off her shoes and reached for the zipper of her dress...damn. It was stuck. She bit her lip, then huffed and padded back to the living room.

"Can you help me out here? My zipper's stuck."

Mac looked up and blinked at her, his mouth falling open. She gave him her back.

"Uh, sure." He rose and moved up behind her, so close his warmth made her skin tingle. His fingers brushed her bare back as he wrestled the zipper free of the fabric stuck in it, and she shivered. The dress loosened around her as he slowly drew the zipper down. "There you go." His voice had deepened to a smoky rasp.

"Thank you." She flashed a smile over her shoulder as she hustled back to her bedroom, feeling oddly hot and quivery. There, she carefully hung up her pretty new dress, the one she probably shouldn't have spent that much money on, but maybe it had been an investment since she may have acquired some new business tonight. She pulled on a pair of soft gray yoga pants and a loose black T-shirt with cuffed sleeves.

Still tingling all over, she sucked in a breath, then straightened her shoulders and marched out to the living room.

"That's better," she announced, sitting on the couch beside Mac. She pulled up her legs to sit cross-legged and reached for her burger.

Mac had taken off his jacket and rolled up the sleeves of his shirt. Her gaze dropped to his forearms and wrists. There was something sexy about rolled-up shirtsleeves on a guy, especially if he had strong arms, which Mac did, darkened with hair. He also had great hands, with long fingers and neat nails.

A little curl of heat wound through her lower belly, and she blinked a few times. First tingling and quivering, now heat curling. What was that?

Okay, she knew what it was. But why now?

"You look much more comfortable." Mac glanced at her. "Although I gotta say, that dress was fucking hot."

She blinked again. "*Now* you give me a compliment. Before, I looked like a Christmas ornament."

He grinned. "You know you looked hot. Guys were checking out your ass all night in that dress."

Then she remembered—so had he. When she'd been bent over looking in the fridge for a beer.

More warmth unfurled inside her. *Hello, lust.*

She took another bite of her burger, chewed and swallowed, and she couldn't help it, she moaned. "God, this is good."

"Jesus. You sound orgasmic," Mac muttered.

Their eyes met. The air in the room changed, going static. Heat washed through her, burning her from the inside out.

She stared at Mac's face, a face familiar to her, a face she'd seen so many times, but now, she was looking at him, and he was beautiful. Male beautiful. Smooth skin with a hint of beard stubble. Dark hair cut short, neat sideburns. An oblong face with a sharp jaw and brown eyes beneath thick eyebrows. And his mouth…chiseled lips, the bottom lip fuller than the top.

She lifted her gaze to his eyes again and saw that *he* was looking at *her* mouth. Now her belly did a full roll of lovely, warm lust.

Whoa.

Their eyes met again, and this time she swore sparks crackled.

With a groan, Mac tossed his burger onto the paper wrapper on the table, snatched hers away from her, and pitched it, too. In the same motion, he reached for her, or maybe she leaped into his lap, because the next thing she knew, they were wrapped up in each other, kissing.

His arms tightened around her, one hand on her hip, the other sliding up her back and into her hair. She twined her arms around his neck and gave herself over to the kiss, his mouth hot and wet on hers, opening her to him. Her lips parted, letting him slide his tongue inside. His big hand cupped her head, tangled in her hair, adjusting the angle to deepen the kiss, and she slid her tongue along his. Everything inside her twisted with excitement, a fierce need pulsing between her thighs with the same beat as her heart. Hot sparks swirled through her bloodstream, and a moan rose in her throat.

Then Mac pulled back, and they stared into each other's eyes. Holy snap, crackle, and pop.

Chapter Four

They dove back at each other.

The kisses intensified, hard and fast and hungry. Mac's hands roamed over her body, and she swept hers along his shoulders, then slipped one hand inside the collar of his shirt to find his hot, sleek skin. He made a noise deep in his throat, and she murmured her appreciation. She curved her fingers around the back of his neck, then over his shoulder inside his shirt, his bones strong, his skin smooth and warm.

His hands on her made her body tingle everywhere, made her ache low down inside. Her breasts swelled, and she pressed them against his chest, needing that delicious pressure there. Then she found herself on her back on the couch, Mac above her, kissing her still, on her mouth, her jaw, beneath her ear. He dragged his tongue along the side of her neck, and she gave a full-bodied shiver of delight.

His hand found her breast, cupping and squeezing it with gentle firmness. Her nipples tightened, and she arched her back, giving a soft cry at his touch. Liquid heat gathered between her legs. God, it felt good…so good. She turned her head and sought his mouth again, his warm, wet, delicious mouth. Their tongues met, and he sucked on hers, then gave her bottom lip a nip with his teeth. Pleasure ricocheted through her, and she dug her fingernails into his skin beneath the collar of his shirt. She needed more of his skin, and she began to work at the buttons of his shirt even as they ate at each other's mouths, kissing with hungry desperation.

She yanked his shirt out of his pants and tried to push it off his shoulders. Big shoulders and arms, thick with muscle. Somewhere in the back of her brain she appreciated that Mac worked out regularly at the gym at the Centric offices.

His hands were spreading magic on her, slipping under her loose T-shirt, pushing it up until he found a breast and again cupped it through her sheer bra.

"Fuck, I wanna see you," he growled and shifted away. His hands grasped her shirt, and she did an ab curl to lift up so he could whip it off over her head.

She bit her lip as he studied her. He gently pressed her back down to the sofa, his eyes glowing with intensity as they moved over her torso, taking in the sheer ivory bra that hid very little. Her skin burned everywhere his eyes touched, nipples tingling painfully, and when he brushed his fingertips over one nipple through the fabric, her body jerked. Another moan rose in her throat, and her eyelids went heavy watching him as he now used both hands to tease her nipples, brushing thumbs, then the edges of his fingernails over them. Streamers of sensation shot to her core, her stomach muscles clenching, and her nipples got even harder.

Mac's face tightened into lines of hunger as he watched

his fingers touch her. He squeezed her breasts again with perfect pressure, and she throbbed even more between her legs. She pressed her thighs together against the intense need.

"Fuck, Lexi, you're beautiful."

Warmth unfurled inside her, and her lips parted as she continued to stare up at him.

He traced his index finger between her breasts, brushing over the inner swells, and she ached for more. A soft sound escaped her lips. Then she watched in a daze as he bent down, his dark head lowering to her chest, and kissed her between her breasts. His tongue licked over the inner curve of one breast, and then ecstasy shimmered through her as he rubbed his mouth over the silky fabric and her nipple. When he sucked her gently into his mouth, dampening the fabric, a hot jolt between her legs had her hips lifting.

"God, Mac!" She couldn't believe this was happening. Couldn't believe it felt so good. And that she wanted it this much. She wanted *him.*

Her body fevered for more. She clung to his shoulders as he nuzzled and licked and sucked at her breasts through her bra and then, thank the Lord, he slid his hands beneath her back to find the clasp and flicked it open.

She wanted it gone, but shockingly, he took his time, using one finger to slide a strap over her shoulder and down her arm, his gaze focused intently on her body as he did. A shiver ran over her skin.

"Your skin's so soft." He brushed fingertips over the upper curve of one breast, then slowly slid the other strap down, lingering on the inside of her elbow. A warm shudder worked through her body. She knew her eyes were wide, gazing up at him, mesmerized by the molten look in his, and she moved her arms so he could tug the bra away. It dropped to the floor, and her nipples stiffened even more.

She waited in burning agony for him to touch her again, aching between her legs.

"Mac," she whispered.

His eyes met hers, and his face came close again. His lips brushed hers. "Right here."

Then he was licking and kissing his way down her jaw again, over her throat, sucking gently at the soft spot at the base. His tongue blazed lower until it touched her nipple. She arched her back, pushing up to his mouth, her eyes now falling closed as excitement built inside her.

Wow, he was good at this. Who knew?

At that point she abandoned herself to the sheer physical pleasure he was bestowing on her as his lips closed around a nipple and tugged. Her womb contracted in delight, and desire sizzled up her spine.

He sucked one nipple, cupped her breasts, then tweaked the other nipple with his fingers, bringing her to a frenzy of trembling need.

"Sweet," he murmured against her skin. "So pretty. Lexi. Wanna make you feel good."

"Oh yeah," she groaned. "Please. Oh please."

His hands went to the folded-over waistband of her yoga pants and inched them down. She helped by lifting her hips and bending her knees. Then she was lying there in her thong panties, and again his blazing eyes were taking her in. The look of appreciation on his face made her skin tingle, her breath go shallow, and her heart tremble.

"You're beautiful, too," she said, and his head jerked as

his gaze shot up to hers. She smiled and touched his hair, threading her fingers through the short strands. "You are. I was thinking that earlier tonight."

"Not beautiful," he muttered. "For fuck's sake."

She still smiled and curled up to kiss his chin. "Are, too. Take your shirt off." It hung open, but he still wore it, and he shrugged it off and threw it aside. Holy hotness.

Then his hands went to his belt buckle.

Were they actually going to do this? God, she really, really wanted to.

"Beautiful," she said again as he stood and shoved his pants down. He had a great body. She'd seen it before, at the beach. Naturally lean, wide-shouldered and narrow-hipped, his workouts had added some bulk to his muscles and defined his abs. Her gaze dropped to the snug black boxer briefs he wore, and wow, they were snug, because he was hard. And big.

She trembled, and her mouth literally watered.

He fell over her, still in his underwear, his body heavy on hers, and she parted her legs to settle him between them. His hands slid into her hair and held her head, and he kissed her again, and again, stroking her tongue with his own. He licked over her bottom lip, sucked it gently, then kissed her more, and she curled her fingers into his biceps, kissing him back until she was dizzy and panting. Her heart hammered, and her skin burned.

His cock was hard and pressed against her sex, and it felt amazing, but not enough. That empty ache needed desperately to be filled. She lifted her hips into him, small pleading noises forming in her throat. She let go of his arms and slid her hands up and down his back. Skin like hot satin.

She daringly let her hands roam lower, over his briefs, and cupped his ass through the soft cotton.

"Damn," she whispered. "You have a nice ass."

He smiled against her mouth. "Was thinking the same thing about you tonight." He brushed another kiss over her lips. "That dress…holy fuck, Lex, your ass was spectacular in it."

"That's a little different reaction than when you first saw me."

"I was holding back. Believe me." He groaned. "Christ, this is insane."

"I know. But good insane. Right?"

"Yeah."

"Feels so good." She lifted her pelvis into him again, her hands full of his tight buttocks. "Want more. I want you inside me."

"Fuck yeah."

Their mouths crashed together, wild and wet. They both made noises, hot, sexy noises. She started to try to remove his underwear, yanking on the elastic. He moved to help her, him grabbing, her pulling, hands knocking, and then they slid off the couch, hitting the floor with a bump.

Lexi paused, blinking. This might be a good time to move to her bedroom…but no. Mac gave the coffee table a shove out of their way, reached up and grabbed the fluffy throw always lying on the arm of the couch, and shoved it under her ass.

Okay, not moving. She was good with that. She reached for him again. On his knees, he pushed down his briefs, finally getting rid of them. His gaze lowered to her panties. She lifted her hips to help him get them off, but shock rippled through her as he gave a sharp tug and ripped them free.

Holy fuck. That was fucking hot. Though she felt compelled to protest. Just a little. "I liked those panties."

He kneed her legs apart and fell over her, both of them now naked. His body radiated heat against her. He kissed her hard, then said, "I'll buy you new fucking panties. A dozen pairs."

All righty. She wrapped her arms and legs around him, loving the feel of his hard cock between her thighs. Heat and pressure built in her lower belly. "Deal," she whispered back. "Just one more thing."

He gave a huff, smiling against her mouth. "What?"

"Condom."

"Hell. Yeah. Got one. Hold on."

It took a few seconds, which was a few seconds too long, but oh well, and then he was back, gloved up.

"Perfect," she breathed. "Now…fuck me."

"My…" He fisted his cock. "Fucking…" He found her entrance. "Pleasure." And he pushed inside her.

She let out a small cry. He didn't get all the way in, he was big, but he kept going, little by little, getting his cock wet with her slickness, and then he was filling her with a delicious pressure. She held on tight, panting for air, arms around his body, thighs tight against his hips. Flames licked over her body.

"Okay, baby?"

"Yes," she whispered. "It's good."

"Fuck yeah," he groaned, then buried his face in the side of her neck. "Lexi, babe. Christ, you feel good."

"So do you. God, so do you."

They moved together. The sensation of his cock gliding

in and out of her was sweet friction, pleasure building deep inside her. Hot. Hard. "Harder," she whispered. Her fingers curled into the nape of his neck, her other hand flat on his back. She lifted her hips to meet his, and it did get harder. Wilder. The small of her back ached, and a warm buzzing began to build inside her. She wanted it, reached for it, squeezed her eyes closed and focused on it, and holy shit, there it was already, crashing over her, stealing her breath. Heat pulsed through her veins. It was fierce. It was beautiful.

Mac rose up to his knees and pushed her legs back, thrusting inside her. She struggled to open her eyes and found him watching her, stark pleasure on his face as he took in her climax and then found his own. With a low, guttural sound he stretched over her again, mouth on hers, and continued to pound into her. One arm slid beneath her shoulders, his other hand pushed into her hair, holding her head as he came, and came, exploding inside her. He pressed his nose alongside hers, his body taut and vibrating.

She held him tight, her heart crashing against her ribs, and his, they were pressed so close together. She gasped for oxygen, dug her fingers into the muscles of his back.

Wow.

They both fought for breath.

"I can't believe we just fucked on the floor," she said, her voice breathy.

His body shook against hers, and he pressed his face into her hair. He was laughing. "I can't believe we just fucked," he said. "You okay, babe? The floor is hard, and I was…rough."

"I'm fine." Her fingers trailed through his hair. "That was hot."

"And fast." He sounded regretful. "Damn, that had been

building up for a while."

She wasn't sure exactly what he meant by that. Had it been a while since he'd had sex? Somehow she doubted that. For her, it hadn't been *that* long. Or did he mean building up between *them*? She pushed those thoughts aside.

"Should have been slower," he murmured, kissing her cheek. "Sweeter."

She moaned. He was turning her on again. "Slow and sweet is nice. But fast and hard is good, too."

"It's all good. Like pizza."

"Hmm?"

"Even when it's bad, it's good."

Now she snorted with laughter, and her arms squeezed him. "That was so far from bad."

"It can be better." He lifted his head and kissed her nose. "You and me in a bed. Let's go."

She bit her lip, and her eyes met his. For the first time, she questioned her judgment. She and Mac were friends. He was her stand-in boyfriend. What was this going to do to their relationship?

How much had they both had to drink?

A rush of warmth surged through her, an urge to hug him and kiss him and lick him all over. Um, what?

Then his cock inside her twitched. He hadn't even gone fully soft and he was getting hard again. His pelvis pressed against hers, where she was still supersensitive and achy, and sparks tingled over her nerve endings, and oh my god, she wanted him all over again. In her bed.

"Yeah," she whispered. "Let's go."

• • •

Mac made good on his promise, making it even better, taking his time kissing and licking Lexi everywhere. *Everywhere.*

Her mouth. God, her mouth. She tasted sweet, and he'd been waiting so long for this. The softest lips, her tongue slick against his as he slid it into her mouth. Sweet and hot.

He tasted her other places, too, running his tongue down the side of her neck, over her collarbone, and then around her nipples. He licked the under curve of her breast, then closed his lips over one hard little nipple and sucked. Jesus, pulling that firm nub into his mouth where it fit perfectly against his tongue felt so damn good. She twitched hard against him, and he loved doing that to her.

He tasted between her legs—heaven, wet and soft. He slid his fingers through silky flesh, then inside her while he licked and sucked, first gently, then with firmer pressure. His brain was burning up, and his dick was on fire. But he was going to make it better for her, not like last time, ripping her panties off, for Chrissakes, and fucking her on the floor. He wanted to make this good for her. He'd wanted this forever.

He made her come again. The first orgasm on the floor had been explosive and fierce. The second one built slower, sweet and lovely, and she came in his mouth with his fingers inside her.

He played with her with his mouth and his fingers, lying beside her on the bed, kissing and sucking her nipples, making her writhe. He brought her up, so close, then his fingers stilled, stroking her lips softly, cupping her with his hand. Then he did it again. When he finally slid inside her, a long, hot slide of pure sex, she was frantic and quivering. He moved over her, holding himself up on straight arms, looking down at her beautiful face, her lust-glazed eyes.

"Touch yourself," he directed.

She blinked. Then slowly she slipped her hand down between her legs and found her clit. Her fingertips brushed his dick, which twitched in response.

"Yeah. Like that." He dipped his head for a lingering tongue kiss. "Make yourself come, babe."

She slicked up moisture, and there was a lot, she was so wet. She circled her clit with her fingertips. He continued to watch her face as she touched herself. Fuck, it was hot. Intimate.

Her cheeks got pinker, her eyelids heavier, and her lips parted as her breathing quickened. The soft, sexy sounds she made drove him crazy. He rocked his hips against her, sliding in and out, the drag of her flesh on his throbbing dick fucking exquisite. His balls tightened unbearably, pressure building dark and swift.

Her fingers worked faster, her head turned to the side, her bottom lip captured between her teeth as she came, her back arching. A groan climbed his throat, and when she let her hand fall to the mattress, he stretched over her to bury his face in the side of her neck. Jesus, fuck, she felt good, coming apart around him, under him, for him. He groaned again, driving deeper into her, his orgasm swelling into a huge, crashing wave. He held himself still, letting it roll over him, breathing her in, her light citrus fragrance combined with the scent of sex making his head spin. She contracted on his cock, wrapped her arms around his shoulders, and he set his lips on the side of her neck.

They fell asleep after that, naked, in each other's arms, in her bed.

When Mac awoke in the morning, he had to blink and mentally sort through memories to figure out where he was. Then it flooded back. He was in Lexi's bed. And they'd had sex. Multiple times.

His insides twisted into a knot. Oh fuck. What had he done?

Had he been drunk last night? He wasn't even sure how many drinks they'd had, starting with the beer at her place, the vodka at the gallery opening, the martinis after. He hadn't felt wasted, but clearly the alcohol had impaired his judgment.

He'd slept with Lexi.

Heat burned over his skin, and he closed his eyes, remembering how things had exploded between them. Shit. He should have put a stop to it. Resisted the irresistible temptation. Which totally made no sense because how could you resist the irresistible? Especially when it was Lexi, and Christ, he'd been fantasizing about this for so many years.

She'd been a willing participant. She'd wanted him, too. And holy mother of fuck, she was amazing—responsive, totally involved, touching him everywhere, kissing him like she couldn't get enough, coming for him sweet and hard.

Maybe… Could she possibly have feelings for him, too?

His chest ached with a desperate longing. Maybe this was what she needed to realize that they weren't just friends… that they could be so much more. That things could be so great between them. Yeah. She wouldn't have slept with him if she didn't feel the same.

KELLY JAMIESON

He studied her sleeping face, her tousled hair, her full, soft mouth, her bare shoulders dusted with golden freckles. Beautiful. He wanted to trace those freckles with his fingertips and his tongue, and look at her forever.

Her eyelashes fluttered open. She blinked at him.

"Lexi." He touched her cheek. "Morning."

"Uh. Good morning." She blinked again.

He rolled to his back. The covers slipped lower as he lifted his hands over his head and did a full body stretch. Then he shifted back onto his side to face her and propped his head up on one hand. "So. What's up for today?"

"Jesus," she muttered. "Look at you all bright-eyed and bushy-tailed. I can barely formulate words."

He laughed. "You need coffee."

"Damn straight."

She lifted her head to look at the alarm clock beside her bed. "Oh wow. It's nearly ten o'clock. I have to work today. I need to be at the Sainsbury Lanes at one o'clock."

"Oh." His mouth pursed. This wasn't going how he'd hoped. He'd been thinking about another round of sizzling morning sex, and then maybe spending the day together. "Okay. What's up there?"

"Birthday party for some spoiled rich kid."

He grinned. "They're paying you, what are you bitching about?"

A smile tugged at her lips. "I'm not bitching. I need the business. I don't make any judgments about parents who spend that kind of money on an over-the-top party for a ten-year-old girl."

"Yes, you do."

She blinked at him.

"Make judgments," he clarified. "You just called her a spoiled rich kid."

"I don't like you in the morning," she muttered. "You're too smart."

He pushed up and kissed her, unable to resist that mouth any longer. "What about tonight?"

"Um. I have, uh, plans."

Unease filtered through him. Why did he have a feeling she was brushing him off?

Chapter Five

"Dinner with my dads," Lexi rushed on, clutching the covers up around her chin. "We're celebrating the success of Papa's cookbook."

Mac nodded. Maybe it was true. She'd already made plans with her dads. He got that.

She waited, her shoulders hunched. He let his eyes move over those bare shoulders…should he push things and reach out and tug that sheet away from her sweet breasts and—

"Okay." She shoved out of bed. "Getting up now." She scooted over to the chair in the corner and grabbed her robe. The view of her backside was spectacular, her ass as fine as he'd always imagined it would be naked. But she completely obscured the view in thick, white terry cloth. She pushed her arms into the sleeves and belted it around her waist, then flipped her hair out. She turned.

"Nice robe." He lifted one eyebrow. *Not.*

She glanced down at herself. She closed her eyes briefly.

"Um. I'm gonna…go make coffee. You want some? No. You don't drink coffee. I can make you something to eat…if you want…then I have to get going…"

She was babbling and clearly nervous. Fuck. Not a good sign.

"Yeah. I gotta get going, too," he said slowly. "Get rid of these contacts. I can sleep in them, but they make my eyes dry."

"I'll make some toast," she said and rocketed out of the bedroom.

Fuck. He flopped down onto his back in her bed. Lexi's bed. Jesus. Burning knives twisted in his gut. She was acting weird, and it wasn't reassuring him that what had happened had been a good thing.

He went into her bathroom to wash up. When he came out, his clothes lay on the bed. Oh, yeah. They'd ditched their clothes in her living room last night in the wild throes of passion, or whatever that was. He slowly dressed, thinking about things.

Okay. She was feeling awkward. That wasn't unexpected. This was a big step for them. He'd just treat her gently, casually, and move things forward slowly.

He sauntered out to her combination kitchen-dining-living room. The odor of half-eaten burgers and fries still scented the air, although she appeared to have cleaned up the food and their abandoned clothes. No signs of their wild sex remained.

Lexi was in the kitchen, leaning on the counter, the Tassimo brewing a cup of coffee and the microwave humming. He finished tucking his shirt into his unzipped pants, and her eyes dropped briefly to his hand inside his fly, then snapped away as he did up his belt.

"Want some zucchini carrot bread?" She pushed a plate across the counter toward him.

"Zucchini carrot? Uh. No thanks."

"It's really good."

"Got any regular bread? Peanut butter?"

He helped himself to orange juice from the fridge while she made him toast and peanut butter, the air in the room leaden. As he sat on a stool at the small counter eating the toast, she chatted away about the fucking weather and her party that afternoon and everything except what they should be talking about.

He finished eating, downed the rest of his orange juice, then rose off the stool. With his insides in knots, he looked around for his suit jacket. There it was draped over the back of an armchair. He walked over and picked it up. As he shoved his arms into it, he sucked in a long breath and let it out, trying to keep his voice normal. Casual. This was no big deal for her. Fine. He'd been acting up a storm for the last six years, he could do it one more time. "Okay, I'm outta here. Good luck at your party. I'll talk you next week sometime."

"Okay. Sounds good. Thanks again for coming last night."

Their eyes met. Normally they both would have laughed at that, and whoever could have said it first would have told the other "mind out of the gutter." Given the fact that he *had* come last night, a couple of times, both of them inside her, just made the air around them go even thicker and hotter.

"To the opening," she added in a rush. Her fingers twisted together. "I appreciate it."

"No problem," he said, shaping his lips into a smile. He leaned down and brushed a kiss on her mouth. Light. Casual.

"See ya later, Lex."

He walked out, closing the door quietly behind him.

Out of her view, he lost the smile. He shoved his hands into his pockets at the elevator, shoulders hunched. Well, shit.

Sex that fantastic couldn't be a bad thing. It had to mean something. Or was he being pathetically optimistic? Slow. He'd just take it slow.

• • •

Lexi had never been so happy to see Vanda.

She jumped up when Vanda walked into the apartment around six on Sunday evening. "Hey! You're home."

Vanda nodded and looked around. "Whoa. What happened in here?"

"I, um, had nothing else to do today, so I did some cleaning."

That was an understatement. She'd vacuumed, mopped the floors, cleaned the windows, wiped finger marks off the walls and light switches. She'd scrubbed every inch of the kitchen, cleaned the fridge and oven, which Vanda couldn't even see. The stovetop, sink, and taps gleamed, the counters shone. Gone were the piles of newspapers and magazines that usually littered the horizontal surfaces. She'd rearranged her bookshelf, tidying it all up. When she'd run out things to clean, she'd made a trip to Pier 1 for some candles and came home with not only candles but new cushions and a gold statue of a monkey in a yoga pose.

"I cleaned the bathroom, too," she said. "You're gonna be impressed."

"Um, yeah. I am."

While Vanda tended to be messy where Lexi was more particular about keeping things neat, neither of them liked cleaning. They managed to put up with each other's idiosyncrasies and usually divided up the chores, but today Lexi had done both her and Vanda's share.

"Looks good. Thanks. Did you eat dinner yet?"

"No." Hmmm. Come to think of it, she hadn't eaten lunch, either. Crap. "Wanna go out somewhere?"

Vanda made a face. "Not really. I'm dragging my butt. Late night last night. Let's order something."

"Okay." Lexi hurried to the desk and pulled open the drawer where they stowed take-out menus. They had some favorite places nearby that they ordered from often. "Thai? Vietnamese? Fish and chips?"

"Yeah, fish and chips. Something good and greasy and salty. I'm going to change, can you order?"

"Sure."

A short time later they were perched on the couch with their food on the coffee table in front of them. Much like Friday night with Mac.

Eeep.

"I need to talk to you about something," Lexi announced.

"Okay."

"Something happened. Friday night. I've been telling myself all weekend that it's no big deal, but I'm kind of worried about it."

Vanda grinned at her, holding a French fry in her fingers. "I figured something was up. You don't usually go on a cleaning frenzy."

Lexi pulled in a long breath, then let it out again. "Yeah."

"So. Friday night. The gallery opening…?"

"Yeah. It was good. Mac came with me, and we had fun. We went out for jazz and martinis after."

Vanda shifted to sit sideways and cross-legged on the couch to face Lexi. "Uh-huh."

"Then I was hungry so…so we picked up food and came back here to eat it and…and we ended up…having sex."

Vanda choked on her French fry.

Lexi's eyes widened. She reached for Vanda's glass of water and handed it to her. "You okay?"

Vanda nodded, coughing. "I'm okay. No need to Heimlich me. Holy shit, Lex. How did that happen?"

"I'm not sure. I'm blaming it on the booze." Lexi waved a hand. "Anyway, the next morning it was a little uncomfortable. I'm worried that things will be so awkward now, we won't be friends. I don't want that to happen."

She hadn't just been worried, she'd been *sick* with worry. All weekend. She'd managed to keep her mind occupied Saturday while she was working, and then when she was having dinner with her dads—after calling and begging them to have her over, since she'd told Mac that's what she was doing. Sunday however, with an empty day alone stretching in front of her, she'd tied herself up in knots thinking about how awful it would be if Mac were mad at her, or things were too weird now to be friends.

"Well. I'm kind of speechless."

Lexi gazed at Vanda, her mouth in an unhappy pout, then sucked in her bottom lip. "Tell me it will all be okay."

"Well, sex between friends does change things," Vanda said slowly. "When you say you want to still be friends…are you thinking friends with benefits?"

Lexi blinked at her friend. "Um. No." She considered that possibility. Her girl parts gave a squeeze at the thought of semi-regular sex with Mac. That could be…good. Actually, more than good. But no. "That wasn't what I meant. I meant, things would go back to the way they were before."

"Can't happen."

Lexi frowned. "That is not what I want to hear."

"Lex, I'm your friend. I'm not here to say what you want me to say. I'm here to give it to you straight."

"You could be wrong. It could happen." She slumped a little.

"Yeah, I could be wrong. I guess. Huh. I need to think about this."

"Okay. Let me know when you have some wisdom to impart."

Vanda grinned. "Maybe we need to rally the troops. Dinner tomorrow night?"

"Yes. I can do that." Mondays typically weren't busy days in the event planning business. Lately *no* days were busy. She sighed.

Vanda snagged her phone off the table and fired off text messages to Mia and Kaylee. "Done."

Her girls weren't much help.

"How was the sex?" Mia asked.

Lexi looked down at her sushi in the Japanese restaurant where they'd met for dinner. "It was epic."

They all gave an appreciative murmur.

"Mac's pretty hot," Kaylee said. "That doesn't necessarily

translate into good sex, mind you."

"The first time was fast," Lexi said.

"First time?" All three girls looked at her with googly eyes.

She poked at a Dynamite roll with her chopsticks. "Well, yeah. Because it kind of…exploded. So it was fast. Wild. Then the second time it was…just me. I mean, he gave me oral." Jesus, that sounded clinical and impersonal. Mac slowly licking her to an exquisite orgasm was so far from impersonal. "Then the third time was slower. And…" She sighed, getting warm inside again. "He's very generous," she finished.

The others all sighed, too.

"Well, there you go," Kaylee said. "Fuck him as much as you can."

Lexi nearly choked on her sushi. "Kaylee!"

"Why not? Nothing wrong with fuck buddies. If it was good, why not?"

She'd been pondering that, too, since Vanda had mentioned the friends with benefits thing. "I don't know if he wants that."

Mia snorted. "As if he would turn down sex. He's a guy."

Lexi pursed her lips. That might be true. "He said he was fine with staying just friends."

"Well, you can try it," Kaylee offered. "But I'm betting now that the toothpaste is out of the tube, you can't put it back."

"That's what I said," Vanda agreed.

Huh. "So it would be like before — I could call him up to be my date when I need one, only after we'd slept together."

"Sometimes you could just sleep together," Mia suggested. "No date required."

She'd never had a "friends with benefits" relationship. But Kaylee had. "That didn't work out very well for you," Lexi reminded her with narrowed eyes. "Remember?"

Kaylee's eyes dropped. "That was my own fault."

"You got emotionally involved," Vanda agreed. "That's just the way women are wired. You have sex with someone on a regular basis, it's hard to not let your emotions take over. That's why friends with benefits usually works better for guys."

"That's sexist," Mia said. "Women can do it just as easily as guys."

"It's biology," Vanda said. "We may have to agree to disagree on this."

"It feels kind of like…using him," Lexi offered. "I like Mac. I care about him. As a friend," she added hastily, with a strange flip in her belly.

"And you're *not* using him as a stand-in boyfriend?" Mia said, raising her eyebrows.

Was she? "I guess I am. But we have fun together. It doesn't feel like that." She paused. "Do you think I shouldn't see him at all anymore?" That thought made her stomach clench hard.

"That's not what she's saying," Kaylee said gently. "If you're friends, and you have fun together, that's good for both of you."

"I agree," she said. "But sex messes up everything." She set down her chopsticks and picked up her glass of wine. "I never thought this hard about Mac and me before. I never thought about it at all. Now look what's happened. Shit." She gulped some wine.

"I say try to go on like you did before," Vanda said.

"Give it a shot. See what happens. Maybe you can still be friends and see each other once in a while."

"Okay." She could do that. She hoped.

They started talking about plans for the upcoming weekend. Lexi normally worked most weekends, since many parties happened on Friday or Saturday, but this weekend she had nothing booked, sadly.

"Awesome!" Mia said. "We're all free Saturday night. Let's go do something."

"There's a hot new club I want to check out," Vanda said.

"Ugh. I don't feel like going to some pick-up place," Kaylee said.

"It's not a pick-up place. They have great music, and we can dance."

"You're the one who likes dancing," Lexi pointed out.

"You all like dancing! Don't you?"

"I do," Lexi admitted.

"How about a movie?" Mia asked.

"I'd like to go out for dinner," Kaylee said. "Somewhere we haven't been."

"Like where?"

This debate went on for some time, and when they parted ways to go home there still had been no firm decision. Also per usual. Sometimes it was like herding butterflies trying to get everyone going the same direction. They were all strong, independent women. Lexi loved her girls.

Chapter Six

Mac resisted the urge to call Lexi over the rest of the weekend and the entire next week. He did send her a few text messages, just checking in, as they often did. Her responses contained many exclamation marks and smiley emoticons. No requests to see him or suggestions they should talk. Apparently she was going to pretend that red-hot sex had never happened.

It made his stomach churn.

On the other hand, maybe he should count it as a win that she was still speaking to him.

Fuck, he was such a loser when it came to her. Was he seriously going to go along with that and pretend nothing had happened, nothing had changed between them?

He wouldn't know that for sure until he saw her again, and the Chicago Blackhawks presented him with the perfect opportunity. It was the last game of the regular season. Since the Blackhawks were already in the playoffs, it wasn't a significant game, but he'd invited some colleagues and clients to the suite. Lexi often came to games with him, helping him entertain clients or business partners. So it wasn't out of the ordinary for him to call and ask her to the Thursday night game, nearly two weeks after they'd done the lust and thrust thing.

Bah. He closed his eyes. It had been way more than lust and thrust. But apparently only for him.

He picked up the phone and made the call, faking calm and casual.

"Hey, Lex," he said. "How's it going?"

"Good! Really good. Super good. You?"

"Great. We hired a new developer this week."

"Good news!"

"Thursday night there's a hockey game. Wanna come?"

"Um…"

Fuck, she was hesitating! His fingers gripped the phone.

"Okay," she said. "Sure. Sounds good."

"I'll pick you up at six."

He ended the call. This was another win. Right?

When she opened the door to her apartment Thursday night, his heart slammed against his ribs. He felt like he was fourteen again, getting up the nerve to ask Chelsea Durban, his big crush, to go to the school dance with him.

Who were they kidding that nothing had changed? *Everything* had changed. He'd seen her naked. He'd tasted her. He'd been inside her. He bit back a groan.

She looked cute in her red Blackhawks jersey over

skinny jeans. He never wore a jersey since he was usually talking business and wanted people to take him seriously, but she always did. Nothing got in the way of her team spirit.

Striving for normal, he slid a hand around the back of her neck, pulled her in, and kissed her forehead. Like he'd done many times. Only this time it took everything he had not to haul her into his arms and start babbling stupid things.

Slow. Easy. Take it easy.

She gave him a bright smile as she stepped away to get her jacket and purse.

Tonight he was driving his Jag rather than using his car service. He had VIP parking at the United Center, which was great so they didn't have to walk miles to get there.

"Who else is coming tonight?" Lexi asked on the way.

He gave her names and a short rundown on why they would be there—besides Pete and his wife, a few lucky employees and their guests, he'd invited two new clients he'd recently signed major deals with, along with their wives, and a prospective client he was currently in discussions with, who was bringing her boyfriend. This was why he liked having Lexi go with him. If they got going on business talk, it was helpful for her to be there to look after the other guests, and also to make sure that the whole night didn't turn into business. Sometimes he forgot about the fun part of the evening, and Lexi had once pointed out to him that inviting clients and staff should be a good social experience for them, not just business. He agreed and liked it when she kept him from forgetting that.

By the time they arrived at the suite, he'd gotten his heartbeat down to a normal pace and relaxed his tense muscles. They'd talked about their weeks, the new developer he'd hired, the calls Lexi had gotten from people she'd met at the gallery opening, the pitch she'd made to Ace Insurance to organize their staff rewards and recognition luncheon, and the progress she was making on the company event she was planning for him, which was taking place next Friday night.

Even though the game didn't matter to the outcome of the season, Lexi was passionate about her team and cheered them on as she always did.

"GO HAWKS!" she shouted at the beginning of a power play.

Mac caught the amused glances some of his guests shot her way. That was okay. They clearly liked her, and she entertained them.

She yelled when the ref made a bad call, cheered when the Blackhawks got the puck out of their zone, booed when a player from the other team tripped a Blackhawk. She made sure people had drinks and food, although there was a small commotion when she somehow knocked over a beer on one of the tables. Luckily nobody was hit, and everyone laughed it off. She chatted her way around the room during the intermissions, mingling and even handing out a couple of business cards. Mac knew this because he had a hard time taking his eyes off her the entire evening. And a harder time staying away from her.

At one point, he moved up beside her to enter the discussion she was having, setting his hand on her lower back. When she said something funny, he smiled down at her. She smiled back, but he sensed the tension at the corners of her mouth. He dropped his hand and wandered over to another group.

He tried to interact with his staff, attempting to give

them some of his undivided attention, especially one of his new employees who was experiencing his first game in the suite. The guy's girlfriend was clearly excited to be there and a little in awe of her boyfriend's boss, which amused Mac, since he still felt like a geeky teenager.

The Blackhawks win put everyone in a happy mood by the end of the evening. He and Lexi said good night to the others, letting them leave the suite first. When everyone was gone, Mac looked at her. They were alone. Fuck, he needed her. So he did what he'd done when he picked her up—slid his hand around the back of her neck, pulled her closer, and moved in for a kiss. This time he didn't aim for her forehead, he was going for her mouth.

She set her hands on his chest. Was she pushing him away? His heart leaped. But then, as his mouth touched hers, she melted into him. His own tension eased, and he kissed her slow and easy, ignoring the heat in his groin. One kiss was all he took. He wasn't about to make a complete fool of himself.

He stepped back, and she stood there with her face tipped up and eyes closed. Then she opened her eyes and blinked.

"Here's your jacket." He held it up to help her put it on.

Encouraged by her reaction to his kiss, he tried not to get too excited. Tried not to think about what would happen when he took her home. He knew what he wanted to happen.

Go for it. She wanted you that night. She still wants you. Do it.

When they got to her apartment, he followed her inside, closed the door behind them, and took his jacket off. She didn't protest. "Vanda?" he asked in a low voice.

The living room was dark, and Vanda's bedroom door was closed. "Looks like she's in bed," Lexi whispered.

He lifted his chin. "Good." Then his hands closed around her waist, and he pulled her up against him. This time the kiss wasn't short. It was long. Long and deep and bone-melting.

"Mac…"

"Mmm." He brushed his mouth over hers.

"What's going on?"

He smiled against her mouth, his nose resting alongside hers. "I'm kissing you."

Her lips curved to match his. "Smartass."

His mouth opened on hers again, he licked inside, and arousal rushed through him, straight to his groin. His tongue pushed gently into her mouth again and again, his hands slid around her waist, her body soft against his. She was turning him on with every press of her lips, every stroke of her tongue.

He should have been smarter than this. He should have been stronger than this. If he was going to do this again, he should've been stopping and talking to her. But he moved her down the short hall with gentle, insistent pressure, and then they were in her bedroom, the door was closed and she was in his arms again and it felt so damn fucking *good.*

She slid her hands up into his hair and kissed him, hot and desperate, pressing against him. When she rocked her hips against his aching cock, his body sizzled with electric shock, then went very still. Jesus. He took one more step until the backs of her knees hit the mattress. She made a little noise as he reached for the hem of her hockey jersey and pulled it off over her head. Beneath it she wore a snug T-shirt, also a Blackhawks one, and he filled his hands with her breasts through the shirt, gently squeezing them.

Oh, yeah. Christ, yeah.

Her panting and moaning urged him on. His blood rushed hotter through his veins as she slipped her hands under his shirt, up over his back. He dipped his head to kiss her jaw, her throat, and her head fell back. With his mouth open on her skin, his hand dropped to the button of her jeans. He used his teeth gently on her, and could feel a cascade of shivers run down her body and her legs tremble.

Her jeans loosened on her hips and slipped lower, and he skimmed his hand down inside them, over the front of her panties. She sucked in a sharp breath. His other hand went up beneath her T-shirt at the back, and flicked open her bra.

"Impressive," she murmured. "One hand."

He couldn't help but smile. "Thanks."

Her pelvis tilted again into him. He knew what she wanted, and gently rubbed up and down between her legs, barely touching her clit. "I'm aching there," she whispered.

Heat rushed through his body. "Good, baby. Want you hot and wet and aching for me."

She moaned. Together they wrestled her T-shirt off. He got rid of her bra, and she shoved up his shirt to bare his chest. He yanked it off, too, and then they were pressed together, naked skin to naked skin, so hot he was amazed there wasn't an audible sizzle as they connected. Their mouths met in another frenzy of long tongue kisses.

"Wanna fuck you hard," he muttered against her mouth. "Make you come. Then fuck you sweet and make you come again. Christ, Lex."

She circled her arms around his shoulders and hung on

tight. He held her with one arm, bending her backward as he reached out his other arm and yanked the covers down. Then he lowered her to the bed. He pulled a condom out of his pocket before whipping off his belt and the rest of his clothing, rolled the latex on, then joined her.

Fuck, he loved it. Loved the feel of her skin, her smooth, sleek legs twining with his, the softness of her breasts against his chest, the heat between her thighs where his cock pressed urgently.

He rubbed his beard stubble over her jaw, and she buried her nose in the side of his neck, breathing in as if she was sniffing him. Then her tongue touched his skin.

His body twitched, excitement pounding through him. He settled between her thighs, slid his hands into her hair, and held her head, tipping it and slanting his so their mouths fit together perfectly. Their tongues slid together, and she sucked a little on him. A growl climbed his throat, dark, desperate hunger rising.

"You taste sweet," he whispered, licking her bottom lip. He nipped at her jaw with his lips, opened his mouth on the side of her neck again, and gently sucked her skin into his mouth, then shifted and kissed his way down to her breasts. "Soft," he murmured, cupping them. "Amazing. Beautiful."

His lips closed over one nipple and her back arched, a soft cry escaping her lips. Her hands came to his head, fingers sifting through his hair, holding him there as he tugged on the hard tip with his mouth.

"Oh my god, I love that," she gasped.

"Mmm. Good." He loved that she loved that. He played with both nipples, tweaking with his fingers, suckling with his mouth. So damn sweet. She writhed under him, and he loved that, too, making her crazy for more. Sensation burned and twisted inside him.

"Mac. Fuck me. Please."

"Oh, yeah." But first he slipped a hand down between them, shifting to the side, and his fingers slid through her wet flesh. He let out a low groan. "That's fucking hot, baby. So wet."

Her hips lifted with greedy need, and he toyed with her there, gently stroking, then settling his fingertips over her clit. She jerked again, whimpered, and made more noises when one of his fingers slid inside her, then returned to her clit. Her body trembled. He kissed her chest, then moved back between her legs, rising onto his knees, spreading them wide.

He lifted her knees, pushed them back, and gazed down at her. "Fuck me," he groaned. "Gorgeous, Lex." The beauty of her body, the way she responded to him, the way she needed him made his chest clench and his dick throb.

"Yes, yes," she whispered, arms out to her sides on the bed. "Oh, yes."

She stared at him, then lifted her head to look at where they were joined. His dick nudged into her, deeper. He gritted his molars, fighting the edge of orgasm, then began to slide in and out of her body. Sensation whipped around inside him, flames burning beneath his skin.

He released her legs and dropped over her, pressing her into the mattress, burying his face in the side of her neck. "So fucking good," he muttered. "You taste sweet."

"Yeah," she whispered. "It's good. You feel so big inside me. Want you deeper."

"Yeah. Hell, yeah." He rocked his hips, harder, deeper.

Giving her what she wanted. What he needed...

"Oh, yeah." She wrapped her arms tight around his back. "There..."

He pushed up, took one of her hands, and guided it to her clit. "Make yourself come, Lex. Want you to come."

She gave a murmur of agreement. He watched her finger her clit, muscles jumping and twitching beneath his skin. As she cried out, he fell over her and covered her mouth with his. She drew her hand away, and he pumped into her faster, harder, his mouth on hers, not even kissing her now, just touching her there. Fiery sensation ripped up his spine, and his balls contracted hard. "There it is," he groaned, pouring himself into her in wrenching pulses, his vision going black, his heartbeat pounding in his ears. He held himself against her for a long moment. "Christ."

Moments later, he shifted partly off her and they lay twined, still connected, damp with perspiration and breathing heavily.

He was a man of his word. That first time was hard. Then he fucked her sweet. Slow. Tender. Sexy. After, they were wrecked and fell asleep in each other's arms, sated and limp.

Awoken by a familiar alarm, he reached out and grabbed his cell phone. He fumbled to turn off the alarm, then slowly rolled back to Lexi and kissed her nose.

"Gotta go, beautiful," he whispered. "It's seven o'clock. You getting up?"

"God, no," she mumbled.

"What time you want your alarm set for?"

She didn't answer for a moment, then finally said, "Eight." She was already slipping back to sleep.

"Done. I'll call you later." He pressed another kiss to her lips, then slid out of bed and dressed. Leaving her sucked, but dammit, he felt good, and they'd talk later. This was all going to work out great.

Chapter Seven

Well. So much for her plan to keep things the way they were. Lexi spent most of the morning beating herself up, something she excelled at. She mumbled self-recriminations as she dealt with emails and mentally flogged herself as she drove to her lunch meeting with a potential corporate client.

She should have had that talk with Mac the morning after they'd slept together. When he'd parked on the street last night and turned the ignition off, her nerve endings had all gone on alert. He was coming in with her. Was he only walking her to her door? Or coming in?

His touches and smiles and then that kiss had made her want more, made her all achy down low inside. If he was walking her to the door, she'd say good night and all would be good. But if he was coming in because he wanted sex… *ack!*

All the way up in the elevator she'd tried to put together a little speech that would basically tell him they couldn't do that, that she wanted to keep their friendship just friends, because…because…why was that, again? She hadn't even been able to think of a good reason. She couldn't in all honesty tell him she wasn't attracted to him "that way" because, holy hotness, it had taken all her willpower not to climb him like a tree and lick him all over.

Then he'd walked right in, pulled her into his arms, and kissed her, and she'd been helpless against it, lust moving through her like slow, liquid heat, pooling deep inside.

She sighed and rubbed her face, pushing away those memories to focus on her business lunch.

After lunch, she broke the pattern of self-flagellation. Yes, she'd been weak when faced with the delicious sexy that Mac was. Who knew the guy was so frackin' good in bed? Seriously! He wanted to "fuck her sweet." Just remembering those words made her quiver. She could hardly be blamed for giving in to that.

They still needed to talk. Except now she wasn't sure exactly what that talk was specifically going to include. Telling him they weren't going to have sex again seemed… laughable.

In fact, there might be a possibility she could become addicted to sex with Mac, because she already wanted more, right now. Huh. Maybe she should go see him at his office… Good god. She stopped what she was doing and put a hand to her forehead as if checking for a fever.

Still. They needed to be clear about what this was. This was sex. Okay, call it "friends with benefits" if they had to name it. She wasn't fond of that term, and was even less fond of "fuck buddies," which seemed more like two people who used each other to scratch an itch. That wasn't what this was.

Why did they have to name it or define it? All she knew was, she didn't have time for a relationship where a man expected her to be available all the time, expected her to look after him by making plans, stroking his ego and...and cooking him dinner. Not that she minded cooking. She actually enjoyed it, and it was way more fun cooking for someone else than just for herself.

Although she didn't have events booked this weekend, she worked hard on proposals for potential clients, who thankfully had started calling again. And she finalized the details of Mac's company event.

"Am I selfish?" she demanded of Vanda on Sunday. "Is it selfish to want to live my own life, to devote myself to my career?"

"Hmmm." Vanda tipped her head. It was her turn to clean the kitchen, and she was mopping the floor. "Yeah."

"What?" Lexi stared at her.

"Well, it is," she said. "But it's fine. It's your life. It should be what you want it to be. If you're not hurting anyone else, then do what you want to do."

Lexi nodded, lips pursed. "Okay then. I still need to talk to Mac."

Vanda turned and fixed a death stare on her. "You haven't talked to him yet?"

"Well, um, I kind of fell asleep the other night, and he had to get up early, and I've been really busy the last couple of days."

She frowned. "Get on that, girl."

"I will. Seriously. Okay, I have a whole day free today. I'll invite him over for dinner and we'll talk. Um...are you home tonight?"

Vanda narrowed her eyes. "I feel like I'm being kicked out of my own apartment."

"No! We can go out for dinner. It doesn't have to be here."

"Or I could hide in my bedroom."

"I don't want you to feel like you have to hide. We're just going to talk."

"How about I go to a movie? Kaylee and I were talking about seeing that new George Clooney movie."

Lexi smiled at her. "Only if that works for you. You can even have dinner with us, if you want."

"Why do I have a feeling you're procrastinating about this talk?"

Lexi gave her a toothy smile. "I've no idea."

She texted Mac and invited him for dinner and got a quick affirmative reply. Great. "Gotta go shopping," she said to Vanda. "Wanna come with?"

"Yeah. We need a bunch of stuff."

She first went onto Pinterest to look for recipe ideas and found a great one for gnocchi with butter and sage, and then a dessert recipe for chocolate caramel shortbread bars. She knew Mac loved gnocchi and also anything with caramel, so these seemed perfect. She lingered over the photo for caramel bacon buns. Mac loved bacon, too. Bacon and caramel might be a hit. She bit her lip. Maybe better to play it safe this time.

They hit Trader Joe's and stocked up, and then she started destroying the shiny kitchen Vanda had just cleaned.

"Thank you!" Lexi called to Vanda as she left for her movie date with Kaylee. "I owe you!"

"Yes, you do! See you later."

The dessert was ready, the gnocchi wouldn't take long, and she had a salad ready to toss, along with some crusty bread to warm. She set about restoring the kitchen to a somewhat clean state, then hurried to her bedroom to get herself ready.

Nerves fluttered in her belly, excitement at seeing Mac mingled with trepidation about the conversation they were going to have.

She left her hair in the messy knot she'd pulled it up into, pieces hanging out of it around her face and neck, but did add a swipe of eye shadow and mascara to her eyes, a brush of highlighter on her cheekbones, and a slick of lip gloss. She stayed in her jeans, low-rise boot-cut ones, and grabbed a loose, flowery blouse in shades of peach and yellow.

The sharp chime of the door made her start as she pulled the top over her head. Mac. She bit her lip, smoothed her top down, and buzzed him in. A moment later he stood at the apartment door.

"Hi!" She greeted him as she threw the door open. "Come on in."

He walked in holding a bouquet of flowers. Yellow and orange gerbera daisies, her favorite colors. She stared at those flowers, her heart tightening. Oh, god.

After a long, painful moment, he said, "Here. These are for you."

She still stared hard at them, blinking rapidly. "You didn't need to bring these."

He shrugged. "It's what you do when someone invites you for dinner. You bring something. Right?"

True. This was true. But he'd never brought her flowers before. She let out her breath. "Yeah, but…it's just me."

At that he smiled and moved closer to hand her the flowers and kiss her nose. "It's not 'just you,' Lex."

Oh, boy.

Still without looking at him, she took the flowers and walked into the kitchen to find a vase. He followed her.

"What's for dinner?" He slid onto a stool at the counter.

She tried to focus. "Um. Dinner. Gnocchi."

"Great. Where's Vanda?"

"She went to a movie."

"Ah." The air in the room changed, beginning to hum.

She pulled a glass vase out of a cupboard and filled it with water, still not looking at Mac. Flowers. He brought her flowers. This was messing with her head.

She set the vase of water on the counter, but as she reached for the flowers, she knocked the vase over. "Oh, shit!"

Mac chuckled as he jumped off the stool and grabbed a towel. "Easy there."

She pulled another towel from a drawer, and they both mopped up the water from the counter and floor. "Damn. Sorry."

"Hey, it's you. I expect these things."

A smile tugged at her lips, but she shook her head in annoyance at herself.

"I was glad you texted me." Mac draped the damp towel on the rack. "Seemed like you had a busy weekend."

"Yeah. You know, the usual." She refilled the vase. "My weekends are always busy. Busy, busy, busy. Friday nights, Saturday nights, I hardly ever have a free weekend evening to, you know, go out on a date, or just stay home or..."

"I know, Lex," he interrupted gently. "I get it."

Did he? Really? Probably not. This needed to be clarified. "What I mean is, I don't have time for a relationship," she blurted out.

The air in the room shifted. She peeked at him as she arranged the flowers in the vase.

"Uh-huh," he said.

She sucked in a deep breath. "Want a drink? Beer? Wine?"

"Whatever. Beer is good."

She got him a beer and poured herself a glass of Moscato. "I'll get the water boiling. Dinner won't take long to put together."

As she cooked, she babbled away about the things she'd been occupied with the last couple of days, trying to act like she wasn't freaked out by a bunch of daisies. Then they both sat at the counter to eat.

"This is really good, Lex," he said after his first few bites.

"Thanks."

He did seem to enjoy it, finishing all the food on his plate and even an extra piece of bread. She wasn't the best cook in the world, but it was gratifying to see him enjoy it.

"There's dessert, too," she told him when he was done.

"Oh, man. What is it?"

"Chocolate caramel shortbread bars. I made them myself." Then she closed her eyes briefly at that silly comment, embarrassed he might read too much into it.

He grinned. "Awesome."

She cleared their plates, then lifted pieces of the sweet onto small plates and added dessert forks. She set one in front of him and then sat to eat her own.

"So," she began, nerves twitching, "I invited you for dinner because we need to talk."

Mac paused with his fork halfway to his mouth. "Uh-huh."

"We should have talked about this after…the first time… we slept together," she continued. "Just to be clear on where we're at."

"Where we're at," he repeated.

"Yes. I was afraid it would change things between us."

His face had gone stony. Blank. "How so?" He took a bite of his dessert, his eyes on her.

"We both had a lot to drink that night," she forged on. "I'm gonna blame what happened on that."

One of his thick eyebrows lifted.

"And, well…hormones. Or something." She twisted her fingers together. "I figured we could still be friends, like we were before, but then…the other night…"

His features were blank, but the air in the room cooled. He gazed at her, swallowed the food in his mouth, and said nothing. "Friends," he finally said.

"Um. Yeah. But then we had sex again. And it was really good!" She hastened to assure him. "Amazing. Now, I guess we're friends with benefits. Right?"

His eyes flickered. "What exactly does that mean?" he asked slowly. "Friends with benefits?"

"It means we're friends. Who have sex. Like before. Just different." Fuck, she was *such* a dork. Uncomfortable with his silence, she kept spouting off at the mouth. "I mean, like I said, I don't have time for a relationship. My business keeps me super busy, and I know you're busy, too. And just because we're sleeping together doesn't have to change anything."

He would want this, too. Right?

For another long moment he said nothing, and she felt more waves of something coming off him despite his face remaining expressionless. Her stomach knotted.

Then he pushed away the plate with a couple of bites of chocolate caramel shortbread bar left on it and wiped his fingers on the napkin. He tossed it onto the counter, then rose off the stool. "Right," he said casually. "No worries, Lex. It's all good."

She stared at him. "Are you leaving? Already?"

"Yeah. Got an early meeting tomorrow, so I'm gonna head out now. Dinner was great, seriously. Thanks."

"Wait! Take some dessert with you. I made this whole pan, and Vanda and I will never eat it. Actually, Vanda will kill me if there's much left because she *will* eat it, and she's always trying to watch what she eats." She jumped off her stool and scurried into the kitchen to wrap up some of the bar in tin foil.

Mac had his jacket on and was jingling his car keys in his hand when she rushed over with the package. "Here. Take these."

His lips curved into a smile, but it didn't reach his eyes. He paused, looking down at her, studying her face. "Thanks, Lexi," he murmured. "See ya."

When he left, the waves of whatever had been coming off him followed him out the door, but the air in the apartment still felt thick, and her stomach clenched. Once again, things weren't going like she'd planned.

She wanted to believe he'd left because of his early meeting, but she was afraid she'd somehow pissed him off. Men! Weren't guys supposed to jump at the chance of no-strings-attached sex?

Whoa. Wait a minute. What if the sex hadn't been that great for him? Was that it? Maybe she'd been so excited she'd missed that he hadn't enjoyed it as much. Come to think of it, she hadn't done much for him. He'd been the one to take control, lead the action. She'd loved it, but there was stuff she could do for him, stuff she was pretty good at, not to brag… She just hadn't had a chance yet. Maybe if they'd done those things he'd be happier.

Her face burned as she remembered telling him how amazing the sex had been, when maybe that had all been one-sided. Shit.

She turned back to the kitchen, her steps heavy as she began to move around cleaning, sliding dishes into the dishwasher, wiping the counter. Her eyes fell on the pretty bouquet, and her throat constricted.

Okay. She needed a new plan. A plan that involved more sex with Mac—one with her being the one in charge and making it good for him. Assuming he ever wanted to have sex with her again, after how he'd left so abruptly.

She nibbled on her bottom lip. Could she do this?

Her plan involved going to his office several days later. She'd texted Mac once, and gotten a very brief reply. She'd also tagged him on Facebook, which had gotten no reply, and her email had likewise gone unanswered. He didn't seem eager to see her, but she was sure a blow job was going to be the answer here.

She knew she was taking a chance dropping in on him at his Centric office on South Wacker, taking a chance that he wouldn't be in a meeting or interview or something. She went late in the day. That way, if things went as planned, they could maybe continue into the evening. Ahem. Around four-thirty she dashed into the offices of Centric—dashing because it was pouring rain outside, and she'd had to park several blocks away.

She recognized Lisa, the receptionist, and smiled at her as she walked in, shaking out her umbrella. "Hi, Lisa. How are you?"

Good to make a personal connection. She'd met Lisa at a hockey game last year when she'd been one of the lucky staff members invited to a game with the head honchos.

"Good!" Lisa beamed a smile. "You?"

"Great. Mac around?"

"Um, I'll check. Is he expecting you?"

So professional. "No, he isn't. I just dropped in, hoping to catch him."

"I'll call him. Hang on one sec." Lisa smiled as she slipped her headset onto her blond head and punched some buttons on the phone. "Hi, Mr. Northrop. You have a visitor. Lexi Mannis." She listened. Lexi admired her completely neutral expression as she replied, "Certainly, Mr. Northrop."

She removed the headset and shot Lexi an apologetic smile. "I'm sorry, he's in a meeting."

Fuck.

Now she didn't know what to do. Was he fucking avoiding her? She narrowed her eyes, and Lisa's eyes widened in response. "He answered your call when he's in a meeting?"

"Um…"

"I'll just go on back." She was being a pushy bitch, but she somehow had a feeling he wasn't in a meeting. He'd been minimally responsive all week, and she was determined to see him. She'd been to his office before, knew her way, so she stalked past Lisa's desk, around a corner, and down the hall.

"Lexi! Miss Mannis! You can't interrupt him…"

Oh, yes, she could. His office door was open, and he was alone. She stopped inside the door, glared at him, and folded her arms across her chest. She tilted her head. "Mac."

He looked up from his computer and jerked back at seeing her. "Lexi. What the—"

"In a meeting, I see."

He actually rolled his eyes. Rolled his eyes at her!

Then she focused closer on his face. His cheeks wore a red stain, his forehead gleamed with perspiration, and his eyes seemed glazed.

She stepped forward, her forehead tightening. "Mac. Are you okay?"

He scowled. "I'm fine. But I'm busy, Lex. What're you doing here?"

"I—" *Came to give you a blow job.* "I came to see you. Are you okay?"

"Fine," he clipped. "Busy. As I said." Then he swiped a hand across his sweaty brow.

She snapped a few more steps across the carpeted floor, frowning. Her gut pinched. "Mac? What's wrong?"

"Nothing. I'm busy."

The blow job forgotten (well, not entirely, but…), she moved around behind his desk. He shoved his chair back, away from her, his eyes looking panicked. Whatever. She touched his forehead. "You're burning up."

He jerked away from her touch. "I'm fine."

"No. You're not. Jesus, Mac."

"I said, I'm fine." Then he got a funny look on his face, turned, bent over, and puked into his wastebasket.

Chapter Eight

Kill me now.

Mac pretty much wanted to die. He felt like he *was* dying.

"Oh my god!" Lexi dropped to a crouch beside him.

"Get out of here," he mumbled, then his stomach rolled, saliva filled his mouth, and he threw up again. Sweat broke out on his forehead and beneath his shirt.

She laid her hand on his back and rubbed a circle. He could feel how damp his shirt was. She touched her other palm to his forehead. "You have a fever," she murmured. "You're sick, Mac."

"Ya think?" He groaned. "Just go away, Lexi."

"I'm not leaving you when you're sick. Come on, I'm taking you home."

"Can't go home," he muttered into the wastebasket. "Got work to do."

"You're sick," she repeated firmly. She snagged a bottle of water from his desk, unscrewed the lid, and handed it to him. "Here."

He took a swig. The water wasn't cold anymore but still washed the vile taste out of his mouth. "Ugh. This sucks."

"Being sick is no fun," she agreed. "You can't function like this. Come on." She tugged on his arm.

Fuck. He did not want her seeing him this way. Wasn't it bad enough he'd completely humiliated himself by reading more into their sex than was really there, by reading more into her dinner invitation than was really there, bringing her fucking flowers, and now puking into his wastebasket in front of her?

His stomach cramped again. Every inch of his skin hurt, and his bones ached. He rubbed his mouth. "Goddammit."

"Let's tell Keyshawn you're leaving," she said, referring to his assistant. She grabbed his suit jacket off the back of his chair, and he let her lead him out of his office.

"Laptop," he mumbled. "Need my laptop."

"Where is it?"

"Docked."

"Oh." She made a face, then kept going. "Keyshawn," she said as they approached his assistant's cubicle. "Could you get Mac's laptop? He's sick as a dog, and I'm taking him home."

Keyshawn pursed her full lips. "Sick as a dog is right," she said. "I tried to tell him to go home earlier."

He wanted to roll his eyes, but his head hurt too much.

"Sit," Lexi ordered, pushing him into a chair. He sank onto the seat, shivering in his sweat-dampened clothing.

She rested her hand again on his forehead. Cool and soft. So nice. He shivered more.

"Let me know if you're going to puke again," she said.

He was not going to puke again in front of her.

Keyshawn carried out the laptop in its case and handed Lexi a plastic bag from beneath her desk. "Just in case," she said. "Get that man to bed."

Mac sighed.

"I will." Lexi thanked her.

"Where's your car?" he asked in the elevator, slumped against the wall.

"A couple of blocks away." She bit her lip. "And it was pouring rain when I came in. That's not going to work, is it?"

"Take mine." He pulled keys out of his pocket with difficulty. "Parking garage, level P3."

She hit another button. The doors opened and closed needlessly at the lobby, then they continued down.

"I have to admit I'm a little excited to drive your Jag," she said. "I never have."

Whatever. Normally he'd freak at her driving his car, but…whatever.

She kept casting worried glances at him as she drove, nudging the plastic bag closer to him. As if he'd puke in his Jag.

She held onto him in the parking garage beneath the Gold Coast high-rise he lived in, all the way up the elevator, then steered him into his condo. "Come on, big guy. Bed."

"If only you meant that in a good way," he muttered.

She smiled.

Rain ran down the bedroom windows in silvery trails, the weather beyond still overcast and gloomy gray. He stumbled to the bed and did a face-plant onto its unmade surface. Relief at being horizontal swept through him. "Roll over." Lexi gently nudged his shoulder. "Let's get your stuff off."

With a groan he complied, and she started unbuttoning his shirt while he undid his pants. Somehow between the two of them, they managed to get his clothes off, other than his boxer briefs. Lexi bit her lip as she helped him undress, then pulled the covers up over him. He huddled beneath them, shivering violently. He'd never get warm. Never.

Lexi pulled the curtains closed, making the room dim and cozy. Okay. Good. That was good. Bright light hurt his eyes. Then she quietly left the room.

He wanted to call her back. He wanted to beg her not to leave him. But he didn't want her to see him like this, shivering and weak and helpless. Christ. His humiliation was complete.

Then she was back. "Sorry, hon, you should take your contacts out," she said softly, sitting on the bed next to him.

He groaned. "Yeah. Right." He pushed up to sit, his aching body protesting, pulled the little discs out of his eyes, and dropped them into the container she held out. Then she left once more. He heard quiet noises, listening for his door to open and close…but soon drifted to sleep. Sleep that was restless and full of bits and pieces of erotic dreams about Lexi.

He had no idea how long he'd slept when he felt her gentle hand on his shoulder. He struggled up from the depths of feverish sleep, trying to open his eyes and focus on her.

"Here. Take these." She had some pills and a nice cold bottle of Gatorade.

"Where'd you get this?" he mumbled, looking at the bottle. She handed him his glasses, and he slid them on.

"Went out and bought it. Got a few things. You haven't been sick again?"

"No." He fell back onto the pillows. "Jesus. I feel like I

was run over by a truck. My whole body hurts."

"Aw. The ibuprofen will help." She stroked his forehead. That felt good. "Want a cool cloth?"

"Unh…"

Moments later she laid the folded, damp cloth across his forehead. He sighed with pleasure.

"You don't have to do this, Lex," he mumbled. "Go home."

"I can't leave you. You're sick."

"I'm fine."

She snorted. "Right." She looked around his room, and he followed her gaze, taking in his shirts tossed onto the chair, underwear and socks lying on the floor, and a crumpled T-shirt on top of the hamper. She smiled crookedly. Bah. She already knew he wasn't a neat freak.

"Drink some more," she urged. He took a few swallows of Gatorade, then lay back and closed his eyes. Now he was hot. He kicked off the covers, rolled to his stomach, and buried his face in the pillow. Sleep came again.

• • •

Lexi left Mac to sleep more. She puttered around his apartment, putting away the things she'd bought. Worry gripped her in tight fists. She'd never seen him like this. He was always strong and healthy and energetic.

After she'd left him earlier, she'd hunted out medications, acetaminophen or ibuprofen, but found nothing in the bathroom, only towels, shaving gel, antiperspirant. And the contact lens solution that had reminded her he should take his contacts out. In the kitchen she'd found beer and a jug of skim milk. For some reason she believed that milk was not good to drink when you were throwing up. It had been years since she'd had a stomach flu, but she seemed to recall that. And beer was definitely not appropriate. He needed some kind of medication to bring his fever down, liquid to keep him hydrated, and something healthy to eat when he felt better.

She'd paused in his kitchen, nibbling her bottom lip, worry gnawing inside her. She needed to get him those things and had hastened out to pick up some stuff.

Gatorade. Ibuprofen. Bread to make toast, clear soup, and crackers.

Now she emptied the dishwasher that was full of clean dishes, then tidied up some newspapers. Luckily her evening was open, which was why she'd picked tonight to go see him at his office. Sitting on his gray leather couch in front of floor-to-ceiling windows looking out over Lake Michigan, she smiled despite her concern for him and shook her head at how her plan had turned out. Foiled again.

Never mind that. The poor guy was miserable. Her heart clenched, thinking about how bad he was feeling, wishing she could make it better for him. She tiptoed into his bedroom and laid a palm on his forehead. Maybe a little cooler. He slept on. That was good.

For a moment, she stood there, watching him. Her heart squeezed. She wanted to slide into that bed and wrap her arms around him and hold him. But he'd probably be more comfortable alone.

Even feverish and sleeping, he was handsome. Stubble darkened his jaw and face around his mouth, now soft and relaxed and beautiful. She slipped a hand through his hair, wanting to feel the thick silky texture. Her fingers lingered, stroking down over one cheek.

Goddamn, she hated seeing him not well.

At one point his cell phone rang, and she rushed to find it and silence it. She did not want him worrying about business. She turned it off. The tech world could survive without him for a day.

She called Vanda and explained the situation. "I'm going to stay here with him," she told her. "Make sure he's okay."

"All night?" Lexi heard the tone in Vanda's voice.

"He's sick," she snapped. "It's not like that."

"Uh-huh."

"Seriously."

"I believe you," Vanda said. "It's just…"

"What?"

"Never mind. Look after your man."

"He's not my… Whatever."

She made herself a sandwich with some of the provisions she'd bought, turned on the television, and found "The Bachelor." She wasn't up on the events this season due to her work schedule, but settled in to watch gorgeous women make fools of themselves and each other over a hot guy.

Mac woke up around eleven. She gave him more drugs and Gatorade. He didn't want to eat anything.

"Go home, Lex," he croaked.

"I know why you're telling me that," she said. "It's because macho guys don't want to be seen as weak and sick."

"Macho?" He narrowed his eyes at her. He looked adorable in his glasses, his hair mussed, beard stubble on his jaw.

"Yes. Don't worry. I don't think any less of you because

you've got the flu."

"Fuck," he muttered. "I was puking my guts out in front of you."

"Must I remind you that is not the first time I've seen you puking?"

He rolled his eyes, then winced. That must've hurt. Her insides tensed in sympathy.

"I was drunk the other time."

"Whatever." She waved a hand.

"Why'd you come to my office, anyway?" He closed his eyes.

"I was going to give you a blow job."

His eyes flew open and his head jerked toward her. "What?"

She lifted a shoulder, giving him a lopsided smile. "I was going to give you a blow job," she repeated.

He choked a little, staring at her. "Why?"

She dropped her gaze to the plaid duvet cover. "I got the feeling you weren't too happy when you left my place Sunday night. I thought..." Ugh. Heat washed up into her face from beneath her shirt. Why did she open her mouth and say stuff like that? "I thought maybe you weren't too excited about the whole friends with benefits thing because the sex wasn't that great for you. I realized I hadn't done anything for *you*. I thought maybe you'd be more on board with the whole idea if...uh..."

"If you gave me head," he finished helpfully.

"Um. Yeah."

He was silent, and she peeked at him through her eyelashes. His mouth was a straight line, his eyes unhappy. Uh-oh.

"Fuck, Lexi. I can't deal with this right now."

"I'm sorry. I shouldn't have brought it up. You're sick."

He sighed. "Shit. Friends with benefits. Seriously?"

That didn't sound good. Her breath constricted in her chest. "Forget it," she said, forcing the words out. "You need more sleep. I'll check on you in a while."

"Go home. It's late."

She didn't respond. She couldn't leave him, even though he didn't want her there. She smiled, turned off the lamp, and left him in his room. They'd talk about it more when he was feeling better.

She curled up on his couch with a soft throw and a cushion. Her sleep was intermittent and restless, which was okay, because she checked in on Mac a couple of times. He slept soundly all night, and when she went in around seven o'clock in the morning, he was walking out of the bathroom.

He was still wearing only snug boxer briefs, low-rise and form-fitting, his naked body all lean and muscled. He stopped at the sight of her. "What are you doing here?" he demanded. "Didn't you go home?"

"No. I checked in on you a few times during the night. How are you feeling?"

"Better. Not normal, but better."

"I'll get you more drugs and something cold to drink. Are you hungry?"

He closed his eyes and shook his head. "No."

"Maybe some toast?"

"Lex." His voice was firm. "Please. Go home."

Her heart stuttered. Hearing those words from him in that tone did not feel good. "I'm just trying to help," she whispered. "We're friends."

"Is that really what you want?"

"What?" Her eyebrows pulled down.

"Friends. That's what you want? For us to be friends?"

"Uh...*yeah*." Of course!

"Fuck." He prowled to the bed and lowered himself to it, covering his eyes with one hand. It sounded like he might have muttered the F word a few more times under his breath. "Okay. We're friends. Now, don't you have to go to work?"

She did. "Yes. Are you sure you're okay?"

"Bring me my laptop. And my phone. Then I'll be fine."

"Are you staying home today?"

"Yeah. Feel like crap, but well enough to get some work done." He dropped his hand to the bed without looking at her. "I'll be fine."

She hurried to get his computer and his phone, also the cold Gatorade and pills she'd promised him. Then she reluctantly left him alone in his condo, taking a taxi back to his office where she'd left her car.

She called him a few times that day when she had a chance, but he didn't answer. Her text message inquiring about his health got a one-word response: *Good*.

At least he was alive.

Business had picked up again, and her week was full with client meetings, researching, planning, and developing proposals and budgets. She also managed to squeeze in a couple of yoga classes. Mac had replied to another text to tell her he was feeling fine, back to normal, back to work. She felt weird about how they had left things and wanted to see him to make sure what he'd said was true—they were friends. Also to make sure he was truly feeling better. She texted him to ask if he wanted to come over and watch the hockey game on TV on Sunday, as the Blackhawks were playing two games away in the first round of the playoffs. She never got an answer.

His lack of response troubled her. Not only was it rude, it kind of…hurt. For the rest of that week, she found herself checking her phone constantly. Her attention wandered in a planning meeting with a new client, thinking about why Mac hadn't answered her. When she learned her dad had got the contract for the building in New York, she found herself wanting to share that news with Mac. She wanted to talk about how she was happy for Dad, even though she and Papa were going to miss him when he was away. But Mac wasn't answering.

Sadness swamped her. Shit. She missed him.

He'd said they could still be friends. They'd gone a week without seeing each other before, and that was no big deal. Why was she missing him this much? Why did her stomach feel like she'd swallowed a rock?

She sent a text reminding him that Friday night was his corporate event. Mac wanted to celebrate with his staff and the big client for whom they'd wrapped up a successful project. He'd requested something fun, and she'd been working on this for weeks.

He did acknowledge that text, with a terse, *See you there*.

This didn't help the hard, heavy feeling in her stomach. She sucked in a breath through her nose and let it out slowly, staring at her phone. Well, at least he'd be there. She wasn't going to make a scene and demand to know why he hadn't answered her invitation to come over and watch the game. Her bottom lip quivered a little remembering that. Maybe she'd have a chance to talk to him, and at least see for herself that he'd recovered from the flu.

Her Friday started early with a trip to the flower market to pick up a bunch of tulips for a business luncheon she'd quickly organized after a phone call last week. She dropped them off at the restaurant, supervised the luncheon, then had coffee with an old friend she used to work with.

After that, she drove to the Platinum Club, where Mac's event was being held, to decorate. The evening was cocktail-party themed, and she'd hired a performance bartender who would dazzle guests with his showy bartender skills and give them bartending lessons. The decorations were classy and simple: black, white, and silver balloons and streamers. The tables were wrapped in black or white tablecloths, each with a huge martini glass centerpiece containing blue and purple illuminated "ice cubes."

Once she was certain everything was set, she went home to change into one of her little black dresses and freshen up for the event. Normally she didn't fuss much about her appearance for business functions, but tonight she found herself wanting to look her best. She hadn't seen Mac since the morning after he'd been sick. He wasn't answering her texts or calls, and she wasn't sure where things were with them. Her instincts were telling her that all was not as good between them as she hoped.

She hated that.

Upon returning to the club, she encountered a minor crisis when she couldn't locate the goody bags that each guest would receive, containing DVDs with bartending lessons, recipes, wine glass charms, and bottle openers. She tried not to let memories of the Jacobs debacle get to her, fighting down a tiny curl of panic. With the help of Platinum

Club staff, they finally tracked down the goodie bags in a storage room where someone had put them for safekeeping but forgot to tell anyone else.

She tweaked the centerpieces, lit votive candles, and adjusted some balloons. Food preparations were well underway, and the bartender was setting up the bar. She dimmed the lighting to the appropriate level, then checked in with the guys working the sound equipment for the informal speeches that would be made after dinner.

Guests started arriving, including Mac's partner, Pete. Everyone was in a celebratory mood and exclaimed over the decorations and the bar. Even though the bartender hadn't started his performance, he mixed drinks with wild antics that made people laugh. Lexi smiled. Making people happy was awesome. She loved her job.

Staying in the background, she kept an eye on things. Where was Mac? He was late for his own party.

Lexi paused in a corner of the room and checked her phone for emails or texts. Nothing. She then scrolled through her checklist to make triple sure she hadn't missed anything. Nope. Tucking her phone away, she surveyed the room, her gaze moving to the open French doors as more guests arrived. Mac. Finally!

She took a step forward but stopped when she saw him smile down at his companion—a woman.

A stunning woman, maybe a little older than Lexi, with long blond hair in perfectly tousled waves and wearing a strapless black dress that hugged her slender body. She smiled back at Mac, and Lexi's insides went glacial as he slid his arm around her waist and leaned in close to say something in her ear.

Chapter Nine

It had been a rough week.

After recovering from the bubonic plague or whatever the hell had struck him down, Mac hadn't felt great the rest of the week. He'd also done a lot of thinking.

He'd been feverish and out of it, but he'd clearly heard Lexi when she'd said she wanted to be friends with benefits.

Friends. Who had sex.

But still…friends.

She didn't feel the same way about him as he did about her. He needed to get his head out of his ass once and for all and accept that. She was never going to love him.

It felt like his fucking heart was being ripped out of his chest and stomped to a pulp, leaving his chest cavity empty and bleeding. He had to deal with this.

He briefly contemplated going along with what she wanted. Maybe just a little longer…maybe she'd be one of those women who'd grow emotionally attached through sex.

Nah, he couldn't keep doing that to himself. It was killing him. Yeah, he liked having sex with her. He fucking *loved* having sex with her. But he wanted more than that. He wanted everything. He wanted more than her sexy body. He wanted her heart. Her love.

Every time they slept together and she disappeared with a cheery wave until the next time would be like a knife slicing off another piece of his heart.

On the other hand, the idea of ending things and never seeing her again made his insides turn to cold stone. Despair filled him at contemplating a bleak future without her, but he had to let go of Lexi. He had to end things entirely.

But he wasn't sure how to do it. Tonight probably wasn't the time or place for that kind of conversation. Fuck. There was no time or place that would ever be right to let Lexi go.

So when Heather Hart, the Director of Marketing with Ruby Inc., with whom they'd just wrapped up the project, had proposed they go to the event together, he agreed. She was smart, beautiful, successful...exactly the kind of woman he should be going out with. She was also single and had flirted a little with him in the past. He'd never been interested because he was all twisted up over Lexi, but now... why the hell not?

He needed to do what he'd done before: date other women in the hopes that one day he'd find someone that would make him forget Lexi.

Now he was at the Platinum Club with Heather, ready to celebrate with the rest of his team and the team from Ruby Inc. He resisted the urge to look around for Lexi, knowing she was there somewhere, and focused on Heather. They mingled with the other guests, making their way slowly to the bar.

Lexi had done a fantastic job.

Of course. He knew she would. She was good at her job. She'd been all torn up about one bad day after that screwed-up birthday party, but he'd always known her business would bounce back.

The decorations looked awesome. Tables had been set up along one wall with various finger foods—meatball sliders, stuffed pepper poppers, shrimp, bacon-wrapped smokies… it was all excellent. Some guests stood to eat at high tables wrapped with white or black cloths, others were having fun ordering exotic cocktails from a very entertaining bartender.

He couldn't avoid Lexi all night. She was directing this bash, and they needed to communicate and coordinate things, and he needed to thank her for doing such a great job. He stiffened his spine and hardened his heart to be able to deal with her.

Before he could seek her out, he and Heather moved away from a group of people, and he came face to face with Lexi.

She'd seen him. He could tell by her face, her eyes big and her mouth tight. She froze in place, her eyes going to Heather, then back to his face.

"Lexi," he said with what he hoped was an easy smile. "Hi."

"Hi." She, too, smiled, a wide smile that didn't reach her eyes. "You made it. I was worried you were still sick and weren't going to make it to your own party."

"I'm fine," he said. "We got…delayed." He looked down at Heather. She smiled up at him, then at Lexi, clearly waiting for an introduction, oblivious to the painful awkwardness snapping between him and Lexi. "Heather, this is Lexi Mannis, from Papillon Events. She's the one who organized this great evening. Lexi, Heather Hart."

"Pleased to meet you," Heather murmured. She stretched out a hand, and Lexi gave it a brief shake.

"I see you're feeling better," Lexi said. "That's good."

"Much better. Everything's going okay tonight?"

"Yes. Great. We'll be starting the bartending show shortly."

"Can't wait."

Heather complimented the decorations and the food. Then Lexi said, "If you'll excuse me, I have to go help with the goodie bags." She darted away.

He watched her go, the sleeveless black dress showing off her slender curves, her bright hair cascading down her back, her spiky high heels tapping across the room. His chest filled with searing pressure.

He made the effort to enjoy the party, watching the bartender tossing bottles and performing amazing feats of mixology, enjoying the astonished gasps and oohs and aahs of the guests. Then some of the guests got lessons, their amateur and awkward attempts at fancy moves making everyone else laugh. He and Pete got up on a small dais with a microphone, thanked everyone for all their hard work on the project, and wished their client much business success.

When he was done, he searched for Lexi, hoping for a chance to speak to her privately.

Yeah. This wasn't going to be easy. But after tonight, he wouldn't have to see her again.

But she must have slipped out early, because he couldn't find her.

The evening was a hit, solidifying the teamwork that had

gone into the project and rewarding everyone's efforts. Too bad when he and Heather left at nearly midnight, he felt like complete crap.

. . .

What the hell? What the fucking hell? Who was that chick? And more importantly, why was she freaked out by seeing Mac with her?

They'd been...*delayed.* Lexi could only imagine what that meant. Ugh.

She sucked in a long breath and let it out.

Get your shit together, Lexi.

Okay. Okay. This was stupid. Mac was her friend. They'd slept together, but they were still friends. She should be happy to see him. She should be happy he had a hot, sexy date. It wasn't as if she'd never seen him with another woman, for the love of cheese. They'd both dated other people over the years. Lots of other people.

Instead she had a tight throat and an ache in her chest. Not to mention a burning in her gut and an unreasonable desire to set Heather Hart on fire. Okay, okay, that was overly dramatic. But still.

She made sure the performance bartender had everything he needed, slipped out to request Platinum Club staff bring more ice, then watched the show along with the others, smiling but not paying much attention. She was glad the guests enjoyed it, which they really did, judging from their reactions, but every ounce of her being was tuned to Mac.

Standing in a corner at the back of the room, leaning on the wall, she watched and listened to Mac speak to the group. He was confident and relaxed, congratulating every-one for their hard work and success, mentioning some people by name to show appreciation for their contributions. She watched his staff listen to him and saw the respect on their faces. She'd seen it that night at the hockey game, too, remembering the new guy who'd been there with his girlfriend and how awed he'd been to be invited to the CEO's suite. To Lexi, he was just Mac. To these people, he was the boss, their leader. And they clearly liked following him. He was magnetic.

This only made her even more confused about the whole evening. How could she and Mac be friends when she felt like this?

Her work there was done. When she'd planned the party, she'd somehow envisioned herself in more of a hostess role, helping Mac, at his side, probably staying to the end to have fun with everyone. Now Mac had someone else there to act as his hostess, and she wasn't needed.

Her stomach plunged and the ache in her chest sharpened.

She collected her purse and her tool kit that unfortunately contained nothing that would help with *this* particular crisis—and left.

Vanda wasn't home when she got there. Lexi poured herself a glass of wine, kicked off her heels, and changed out of her dress, then sat on the couch with her bare feet on the coffee table and watched a movie. Her body ached, her stomach hurt, and her eyes were watery. Probably she was coming down with that damn flu Mac had had.

Yeah, that was it.

"He was there with a date," Lexi told Vanda the next morning, sitting at the counter in their small kitchen, picking at a Morning Glory muffin from Trader Joe's. She hadn't thrown up but still felt blah. Maybe it was a weaker version of the flu. "A gorgeous blonde."

Vanda gave her an odd look. "Really?"

"Why do you seem surprised?"

Vanda's mouth kind of puckered up, and her eyebrows slanted down. Then she shrugged. "I thought after you guys slept together, things would change."

"I know. You said that. I told you he was fine with staying friends."

"So you should be happy he was on a date."

"I know I should be. But I'm not. Because I'm a crazy, messed-up bitch."

Vanda burst out laughing. "Right."

"Seriously. I don't know why it bugs me this much. He's dated other girls."

"When was the last time he had a girlfriend?"

Lexi had to think about that. "I can't remember. It might have been when I was in Europe."

"That was two years ago."

"Yeah." She squinted, still thinking. "He's gone out with other girls. I can't say I ever got to know any of them, but I know he has."

"That's probably what this is."

Lexi didn't really want to say she knew that and it didn't make her feel any better. "I think the problem is, he never told me," she finally said. "He never answered my texts or calls last week, other than to say he'd see me at the party. Before, if he had a date with someone, he would've told me."

"Ah."

"Therefore," she continued, "it means our friendship *has* changed. Exactly what I was afraid of." And there it was. That was the problem. She stared morosely into her mug of coffee, stomach still queasy.

"Call him," Vanda suggested. "Ask him about her."

"I can't do that!"

"Why not?" Vanda lifted an eyebrow. "If he would have told you before, why not talk about her now? You want things to stay the same."

This was true. "You make too much sense," she grumbled. "I'm going to do some yoga."

"You can call him after."

"Sure."

Yoga was her go-to way to work through problems. After that she had to get ready for another party, a charity event she'd helped plan, not charging her usual fees. It was Girls' Night Out, a silent auction of donated designer shoes and handbags, a fashion show, with cosmos and finger foods. Vanda, Mia and Kaylee were all going, too.

Parties, parties, parties. A life of never-ending parties sounded great, but for the first time since she'd started her business she kind of wished for a Saturday night at home, maybe curled up on the couch with someone watching a movie and eating popcorn and drinking root beer. Someone like Mac.

The last thing she felt like doing was going to a party.

She soon abandoned the yoga and lay flat on her back on her mat, staring up at the ceiling, worry circling inside her about why she was so troubled about Mac dating Heather.

Their committee had rounded up lots of volunteers to work this Girls' Night Out event, so there wasn't much to do, meaning the committee, including Lexi, could partake of the cosmos and food, and drool over Christian Louboutin and Valentino shoes, and Coach and Michael Kors handbags. Since it was for a good cause (women's cancer research), she put a few bids in, although she'd have to see how high the bidding went before she decided if she was actually going to go for those sweet leopard-print Manolo Blahniks.

They watched the fashion show, sipping drinks and exchanging comments about the lovely outfits. After that, they sat on loveseats arranged around the room and drank more cosmos and gossiped and laughed. Well, everyone else laughed.

"What is wrong with you tonight?" Mia asked. "You're so quiet. You're not usually quiet. Ever."

Lexi gave her a half smile. "Gee, thanks."

"You're still thinking about Mac, aren't you?" Vanda asked.

Lexi sighed. "Yeah."

"Why? What happened?" Kaylee's eyebrows pulled together.

Lexi told them about Mac bringing that girl to the party last night. Unfortunately as she talked, she got kind of agitated and ended up wearing some of her cocktail.

Mia wordlessly handed her a wad of napkins. Lexi dabbed at the wet spot on her dress.

"Did you call him?" Vanda asked.

"No."

Vanda gave her a slitty-eyed look.

"I'll call him now." Lexi set her glass and the napkins on the table and reached for her purse.

"Now?" Vanda and the others all exchanged looks.

"Yeah. Now."

"Um, you've had a few drinks, Lex," Vanda pointed out. "Also…"

Lexi ignored her. She swiped her screen and found Mac's number and called him. It took three rings. Maybe he wasn't going to answer… Then his deep voice came on.

"Hey, Lexi."

"Hi! Um. I didn't get a chance to talk to you much last night. Did you have fun?"

She heard a lot of background noise before he answered. Where was he? Probably on another date with Heather. Her heart plummeted to her toes. Shit. Why hadn't she thought of that?

"Yeah. It was nice. You did a good job, Lex."

"Thanks."

"I was looking for you—I wanted to talk—but you'd already left."

He was?

"Um, yeah. My work was done. What did you want to talk about?" She bit her lip, her insides fluttering wildly.

Loud noise in the background made his reply inaudible.

"I shouldn't have bothered you," she said quickly. "Sounds like you're busy." She paused, then said, "Are you—" Her throat closed up. She cleared it. "Are you seeing Heather?"

Mac was silent, more background noise in her ear. "Lex."

At that moment, Lexi's phone was plucked from her

hand by Vanda, who spoke into it. "Hi Mac, this is Vanda."

"What are you doing?" Lexi grabbed for her phone back.

Vanda ignored her. "Yeah. Where are you? Uh-huh. Yeah. For sure." She gave Lexi a look, then said, "Okay. I'll tell her."

She ended the call, tossed Lexi her phone, and said, "He's on a date."

"With Heather?"

"Yeah."

Lexi went very still. Her head felt heavy. Her lips pushed out. "Damn," she whispered.

She sensed everyone's tension, the air humming a little as they made small noises and exchanged glances.

"What's going on, Lexi?" Kaylee asked.

"You don't like it that he's dating someone," Vanda noted.

She wasn't wrong. "No," Lexi admitted sadly. "I'm confused."

"I see that. But I think it's clear what's happening."

"What?"

"He got tired of being used."

Vanda had said that to her before, about using Mac. "I don't use him," she protested. Then she considered that. "Do I?" She looked at the other girls for answers.

"I guess it's how *he* feels that matters," Kaylee said slowly. "If he felt used, then yeah, that's a problem."

"Give me my phone." Lexi wiggled her fingers. "I'm going to call him back right now."

"No, you're not. This is not the time for this. At least wait until tomorrow. For one thing, you're a little drunk, and for another, he's on a date."

Vanda was right. She needed to do some long and hard thinking about her and Mac and their relationship. Mostly about herself, though, and why she was so mixed up about this.

"Do you like him as more than a friend?" Kaylee asked softly.

Yeah, that was what she *didn't* want to think about. Her feelings for Mac. She'd been trying not to think about that for weeks.

"Yeah." She blew out a breath. "I didn't think so, but seeing him last night with that girl…it really bugged me. I think I might be…jealous." She looked at her friends. "Which means I do care about him as more than a friend… doesn't it?"

"I'm gonna weigh in on the 'hell yeah' side of that debate," Mia said. "Honestly, Lexi, we've all wondered about that for a long time."

"Really?" She frowned.

"Really. You two actually make a great couple."

Lexi's eyebrows flew up at that.

"Or maybe you just want what you can't have," Mia added.

Yeah, that made her sound like a great person. "He's had girlfriends before. I was never jealous of them."

"Once again, that was a couple of years ago," Vanda pointed out. "And you hadn't slept with him then."

Later that night, in her bed, in the dark, Lexi got her chance to think about what her friends had said. They were making her think about things she didn't want to, things about herself she didn't want to see.

She hated the idea that she'd been using Mac. Or that

he might have felt used. Because while she'd admitted it was nice to have him as a stand-in boyfriend, she'd never intended to use him. Hadn't they both enjoyed the time they spent together?

Seeing him with another girl made her want to punch something. The burning feeling that rose inside her fucking stung. Yeah. She was jealous. It wasn't pleasant. She wanted to pound her pillow. Throw things against the wall. Scream out loud.

She did none of those things, but the burning feeling continued to spread through her veins.

Could it really be just that she wanted something she couldn't have? Like Kaylee, who kept falling for married men. For some reason, to her the idea that a guy was taken made him much more attractive. They'd analyzed that one to death and concluded that a guy's hotness did in fact increase if another girl showed interest in him, somehow making him more worthy. Surely she hadn't been sucked in by that?

She flopped to her back and stared into the darkness. Damn. Was she actually that shallow? And selfish? Selfish and shallow. No wonder Mac didn't want to be friends with her. Or friends with benefits. Or anything.

That made hot moisture gather in the corners of her eyes.

Talking to her girls was good, but at that moment, she needed to talk to Papa. Tomorrow was Sunday, and she was going to go visit her dads.

Chapter Ten

She would only talk to Papa about this. Dad was different. He'd been unhappy when she'd started going out with boys when she was a teenager, and probably would have forbidden dating until she was thirty, except she'd told him, "Nobody dates anymore, Dad. We just hang out."

But she *had* talked to Papa about the boys she liked, and he understood.

She called to see if they'd be home that afternoon. They confirmed they would, thrilled that she was coming over. They both liked to cook and were always trying out new recipes in their fabulous kitchen, so they told her to come for lunch. A while later, she sat with them at the big granite island, eating roasted tomato and basil soup with fresh homemade croutons and then croque monsieur sandwiches that melted in her mouth.

"Yum," she said. "I want to learn how to make this."

"I didn't think you had time to cook," Dad said.

"I don't," she admitted. "When I have time, I do enjoy it." She remembered the meal she'd made for Mac last weekend.

"What's wrong?" Papa asked.

She blinked at him. "Wrong?"

"You looked so sad. Is everything okay, princess?"

His concerned expression made her throat close up. She set down the last bit of her sandwich and blinked rapidly at her plate. "No."

"What's wrong?" He shifted closer and reached out to lay one of his hands on hers. "Work problems?"

"No. Work is good. Things have picked up again." She told him how the woman he'd introduced her to at the gallery had in fact hired her to plan her parents' fiftieth wedding anniversary party.

"That's fantastic. So what's the problem?"

She glanced at Dad. "It's…Mac."

They both frowned. "Mac? Your friend Mac?"

"Yes." She bent her head and sighed. Probably not many girls discussed their sex lives with their fathers. If she started talking about sleeping with Mac, Dad would freak.

"What did he do?" Dad demanded.

Yep, there it was. "Nothing. I'm just kind of confused about what's happening with him."

"I don't think I want to hear this," he muttered, clueing in. He slid off his stool and began clearing dishes away. "Why don't you two go into the den and talk."

She shot him a grateful smile. "Thanks, Dad."

She and Papa moved into the den. "I'll fill him in later," Papa said with a gentle smile. "What he needs to know, that is."

"I know you will." They sat on the couch, and she picked up a cushion and hugged it, sitting sideways, her back to the armrest.

"Tell me what's going on."

She sighed. "Okay. Things have gotten complicated between Mac and me."

He frowned. "How so?"

"Well, we were just friends, and then…"

His eyebrows lifted. "Oh." He tapped a finger to his chin. "Took him long enough. That man is crazy about you."

Lexi bugged her eyes out at him. "What? No he isn't."

"Oh yeah, princess. He is. The way he looks at you…the way he treats you. I've watched him. Your dad has noticed, too, although he wanted to take Mac somewhere and rough him up so he'd never lay a finger on you. I talked him out of it."

"Really?" Thoughts rattled around in her head for a moment, and she couldn't get hold of a single one and make sense of it. Dad and Papa had thought Mac was crazy about her?

"What's complicated?"

"Well." She tried to focus. "I told him I didn't want things to change between us, and we could still be friends."

Papa's eyebrows shot into his hairline, but he said nothing.

"I thought we could," she continued. "We kept doing what we usually do, but…things did get weird. Then he got sick. He had the flu. I went to see him and ended up taking him home and looking after him."

"That sucks," he said. "He's okay?"

"Yeah. He's better. And then…" She sucked in a breath. "It was his big corporate event Friday night, and he brought…another girl."

"Oh, no." Papa's eyes shadowed. "It wasn't his sister or something?"

"No. He introduced me to her. They were on a date together. And I discovered that I was…jealous." Papa's grin baffled her. "What's so funny?"

He shook his head, still smiling. "I see why you're confused."

She squeezed the pillow. "I think…I think I'm in love with him." She met Papa's eyes and his face was a little blurry. "But it's too late. He got tired of me using him and moved on to someone else." Saying the words made her lungs burn and her throat clog up.

"Using him?"

She swallowed hard so she could speak. "That's what Vanda said. She thinks I use him and he's tired of it."

"Use him how?"

"Well, we kind of joked around and called him my stand-in boyfriend. I could invite him to go out when I didn't have a date. Like the gallery opening that night."

"But don't you go to hockey games with him in his suite?"

"Yes. Do you think that's taking advantage of him?"

"Uh…*no*. He invited you, right? And from what you've told me, it sounds as though he likes having you there to help entertain clients."

"Yeah, I think he does."

"How is that taking advantage of him?"

She shrugged and plucked at the cushion. "I guess it isn't. But I asked him to help me build my IKEA bedroom furniture. I made him dinner for doing it. I never intended to use him! I have fun when I'm with him. I thought he did, too.

I feel horrible if he thought I was taking advantage of him."

"I don't think that's the case," Papa said slowly. "But maybe you should ask him. That's the only way to know how he feels."

She made a face. "It's too late now."

"It's never too late," he said gently.

"Do you think I'm too selfish to have a relationship?" she blurted out.

He gave a huff of laughter and shook his head slowly. "Of course not. You are not a selfish person, princess. That's the last word I'd use to describe you."

"I've never had a long-term relationship," she said. "Hector, but that didn't last long. He got tired of me working all the time."

"*Phhht*. Good riddance." Papa waved a hand.

"I do work a lot. And I like to have time for myself. And for my friends. Boyfriends always seemed like a lot of work."

He nodded thoughtfully, then said, "All relationships take time and work, sweetie. If you want it enough, you make it a priority. Doesn't sound like any of those other guys were important enough for that."

"Um. I guess not." His point had merit.

"Did Mac seem like a lot of work?"

"He wasn't a boyfriend."

Papa lifted his chin. "Did he?"

"No." The answer came immediately to her lips. Of course not. It wasn't work. It was fun. She liked being with him, doing whatever it was, even if it was building furniture, complaining about the instructions, and killing themselves laughing when they built a drawer completely wrong.

"Even when he was sick?"

She swallowed hard. Still no. "I wanted to take care of him and make him feel better," she said in a small voice. "I was worried about him."

"Princess. You *are* in love with him."

Her bottom lip quivered, and her eyes filled with tears. "I've messed everything up." She swiped her forefinger beneath one eye to catch the drips. "*Now* I figure it out, when it's too late, and he's with someone else."

"Maybe. But that doesn't mean it can't be fixed. I stand by my opinion that he feels the same about you."

"What about Heather?" she asked bitterly. "Pretty, blond Heather."

"Go fight for him."

She sucked on her bottom lip. "I'm afraid. What if he doesn't feel that way? What if he doesn't want me?" The idea of spilling her guts and being rejected by him made her insides cramp painfully.

"I think you two have something great together," he said gently. "But it takes courage to put yourself out there. No doubt about that." He smiled. "But cowardly is another word I would never apply to you. Remember when you were about sixteen, you had a big crush on that kid…what was his name…Jason?"

"Yeah…"

"Then he finally asked you out to a movie and said he'd pick you up, but he never showed, and you were devastated?"

Yes, she definitely remembered that experience.

"Turned out his dad wouldn't let him come to our house because you had two gay men as parents."

That memory made her blood scald her veins and her teeth grind. "I remember."

"When you found out, you went over to his place, knocked on the door, and when they let you in, you tore a strip off Jason *and* his dad and told them there was no way in *hell* you would ever have anything to do with someone who came from a family with those kind of values, and how glad you were that *your* parents were raising you to treat everyone with dignity and respect, and a family isn't determined by the gender of the people but by the love and commitment they share."

She grinned. "That was good, wasn't it?"

"It was magnificent. We were never so proud of you."

Warmth expanded in her chest, and she smiled at Papa. "Especially since two years before that, I wanted to run away because I *hated* having two dads."

His eyes softened. "Every teenager hates their parents at some point. And that wasn't the only time you had to be courageous like that. We questioned ourselves, whether it was the right thing to do, to bring up a child in that environment, knowing the challenges you'd have to face. Lex…have there been other times where the men you've dated have given you a hard time about your family?"

She blinked. Uncertainty settled in her chest. There were some things she never wanted to tell her parents. "Maybe a few," she whispered.

"Huh. So there have been."

She made a face and gave a tiny shrug. "They were never worth it anyway."

His eyes crinkled up. "Shit. Princess, don't let that stop you from having a relationship."

She frowned. "I would never let that stop me from anything."

"Okay. Good. You've faced a lot of challenges because of us, and every one of them you met head on."

She choked on a little sob. "God, I love you, Papa."

"Love you, too, princess. Think about that, okay? Now… you have another challenge. And I have faith in you that you can meet this one, too."

"But I don't know what to do!"

He smiled. "You will. You think about being brave and standing up for what you believe in. Because you may have some doubts about yourself—but I know you believe in love."

Tears spilled out of her eyes, but she still smiled at Papa. "I do."

She'd seen love and commitment with her dads, who'd been together longer than some of her other friends' parents. Her dads, who not only loved each other but loved her too, unconditionally. But until now she'd never realized how scary love was, how vulnerable it made you. And possibly even more so for them. Yeah, they were good role models.

After Dad and Papa took her for ice cream, she went home. The apartment was empty, and she was glad, because she needed some alone time.

She changed into a pair of cropped yoga pants and a tank top, started her yoga playlist on the sound system, then rolled out her mat on the living room floor. She went through the sun salutation and moved on to the butterfly, which was supposed to be good for grounding and calming.

Papa's story about Jason ran through her head, followed by memories of some of the other guys she'd dated, guys she'd thought she cared about who couldn't deal with her two dads. She'd kicked them to the curb without hesitation, not wanting anything to do with someone who couldn't accept that. But…maybe it had made her a little gun shy. Had she been protecting herself by being too busy for a relationship?

Except, really, she'd been *in* a relationship, with the greatest guy in the world, a guy who'd completely accepted not only her and her spilling of drinks and lack of IKEA skills but also her gay parents. She just hadn't realized it. And she'd blown it.

She cursed herself, her stupidity, her horrible timing. Why didn't she figure this all out last weekend? *Before* Mac started dating someone else. It still would have been scary telling him how she felt, but way less than now. In fact, telling him now seemed incredibly presumptuous and…well, icky. He was with someone else. Why would she tell him that she'd suddenly discovered she was in love with him? Who would do that to someone else? Why would she put him in that kind of awkward position?

But what if Papa was right? What if Mac *did* have feelings for her?

She moved on to downward dog. Ed Sheeran's soulful voice sang about love, and anguish squeezed her lungs, stiffening her in the pose. She closed her eyes and tried to breathe.

What made Papa think Mac was crazy about her? She hadn't seen any signs. Perhaps he was mistaken. He was her father and he loved her. Naturally he thought everyone loved her. Or something like that.

Then as she finished her pose, her eyes fell on the flowers. The ones that still sat on their little dining room table, the bright gerbera daisies starting to fade and droop.

Mac had brought her flowers. Her heart clenched. She

sat down hard on her butt, still staring at them.

Had he thought her dinner invitation was something more? Was that why he'd brought her flowers?

A wave of pain washed through her, so intense her breath whooshed out and she doubled over. She covered her face with her hands. Oh god. What had she done to him?

Could she go tell him how she felt?

The door opened and Vanda walked in. Lexi straightened, crossing her legs into lotus position. "Hey," she said, no smile.

"Hey. You're back. Have a nice visit with your dads?"

"Yeah. I had a good talk with Papa." Lexi paused. "Do you really think I'm selfish and was using Mac?"

Vanda tossed her purse onto a chair and sat on the coffee table in front of her, leaning forward. "No."

Lexi eyed her. "Then why'd you say those things?"

"I was trying to open your eyes."

"Oh." She pursed her lips. "Well, I think it worked."

Vanda tipped her head to one side. "Oh yeah?"

"I finally figured out that I actually have feelings for Mac."

Vanda smiled. "It's about fucking time. Yay!"

Lexi scowled back at her. "No! Not yay! He's seeing someone else! I figured it out way too late."

Vanda shook her head. "It's not too late."

"That's what Papa said. But how can I go tell him *now* how I feel?"

"He wasn't with Heather last night."

Lexi's mouth fell open, and she stared at her. "What?"

"You'll probably be pissed off at me, but when I took your phone last night I asked him. He wasn't out with her."

Lexi gasped. "You lied?"

"Yep. I did. But if you don't get your head out of your ass and sort things out with him, it's highly likely he *could* end up with Heather or some other chick." Her eyes softened. "I think you still have a shot."

Something huge and breathtaking swelled up inside Lexi. Oh god. "Really?"

"Yeah. I've thought all along he cares about you. Seriously, Lex. I think there's something there. I'm just glad you finally figured out how you feel."

"I'm terrified."

"I know. Maybe you should go see him."

Her stomach tensed, as did her muscles. So much for yoga. She rolled to her back, flat on the floor, staring at the ceiling. "You lied to me, you bitch."

"Yeah. You'll forgive me."

"Probably." She rolled her head to the side, and they smiled at each other.

Then she jackknifed up. "He wasn't with Heather."

"Right."

She closed her eyes, curled her fingers into her palms, and took several fast shallow breaths. "Okay. I have to do this."

"You go, girl."

"What if he's not home? Should I text him? Call him?"

Vanda grimaced. "Hell if I know."

Lexi narrowed her eyes. "You seem to know a lot about what I should be doing. Help me out here."

Vanda grinned. "Well, I don't think it's ever good to tell a guy you love him by texting him. And probably not over the phone, either. Unless you're in a long-distance relationship and that's the only option. Though Skype would be better."

"Vanda!"

"Go. Go over to his place. If he's not there, try calling or texting to find out where he is. One step at a time, girl."

"I like to plan things. I like to know what's going to happen." She sucked in air. "I think I'm hyperventilating."

"You aren't. Go."

She looked down at herself. "I should change."

"You look fine."

"Yoga clothes? Seriously? This is important."

Vanda laughed. "Oh my god, Lexi, quit procrastinating! As if your clothes matter right now."

She had a point.

"Okay," Lexi said. "I'm gonna do this." No more stalling. No more second-guessing. Even if she ended up broken-hearted and humiliated, at least she'd have her answer. She'd know. That thought made a knife twist in her chest and her legs go weak, but she ignored it and grabbed her purse and car keys. She drew in a long breath, lifted her chin, and met Vanda's eyes. "Wish me luck."

Her face softened. "Good luck, sweetie. You can do this."

Of course she could. She smiled and held her head high and her shoulders back as she walked out. In the hall, she paused to slump against the wall, her stomach churning. She couldn't do this.

Then she remembered Papa telling her how brave she was. He and Dad had something beautiful and amazing. She wanted love like that for herself. She wanted Mac in her life. He was worth the risk.

Last time she'd gone to surprise him it hadn't worked out very well. He'd puked in his garbage can. She had to smile. Poor Mac. He hated being sick, and he'd hated being so weak in front of her. But that didn't matter to her. She knew how strong and smart and in control he was.

She had no idea how this was going to go and was terrified out of her mind, but she had to do it. She straightened and headed to the elevator.

Chapter Eleven

Mac finished his shower and rubbed his jaw as he studied his face in the bathroom mirror. Nah, he wouldn't bother shaving.

Naked, he walked into his bedroom. He'd slept in late, and now felt grouchy and restless. He threw himself down on the bed, his hand going to his junk. Maybe a little hand action would improve his mood…

Then his phone rang. He ignored it. It kept ringing.

Shit. He rolled over and grabbed it off the nightstand. Caller ID told him it was the doorman downstairs. He frowned. Someone was there? He didn't want to see anyone. He didn't want to talk to anyone. He was busy. He tossed the phone down. Then he sighed and picked it up and answered.

"There's a Lexi Mannis here to see you, Mr. Northrop."

Argh. Lexi. Great timing. He was lying there naked and no doubt the hot fantasies he was about to indulge in were going to involve her. She was the last person he wanted to see.

What was she doing here? Was she going to try to once more convince him they could be friends? Fuck that bullshit. He was done. Now he was going to tell her that.

He closed his eyes and sighed. Maybe this was for the best. He owed it to her to tell her to her face that they couldn't be friends. They couldn't be anything. Finally, he said, "Okay, send her up."

He dropped his phone, then knifed up and off the bed to grab the jeans he'd worn yesterday. When he'd pulled them on, he yanked a clean T-shirt out of a drawer and dragged it over his head, then headed to the door, arriving just as Lexi knocked. He jerked the door open, the adrenaline in his bloodstream putting a little too much force into it. One arm on the door, he gave her what he hoped was an impassive look. "Hey. Come in."

She walked in past him, heading straight into his living room, and without waiting for an invitation, collapsed onto his couch.

He closed the door and followed her with one eyebrow raised. "Everything okay?"

"No."

He sprawled out at the other end of the couch. "Hung over?"

She frowned. "No. Why do you say that?"

"You sounded a little lit up when you called last night."

She blinked. "Um. Yeah. I'd had a few cosmos. But I wasn't that drunk! And I'm not hung over."

"Okay, good. What's up?"

She rubbed her mouth. "I don't know where to start."

His eyebrows pulled in toward his nose. "Can't help you

out, babe. I'm clueless until you clue me in."

"Well. Remember when I said we could still be friends?"

"Yeah." His mouth compressed, then he forced it to relax. "Several times."

"Yeah. Well, I was wrong."

He wiped all expression off his face, but his body tightened. "How so?"

"I mean…" She took a big breath. "I think my feelings have changed for you. I don't want to be friends anymore."

His gut cramped. Even though that was what he fully intended to tell her, it fucking sucked to hear it from her. It was okay, though. He could handle this. "Really," he said, not moving a muscle. "And what brought on this realization?"

She swallowed and clasped her hands tightly around one knee. "I don't mean I don't *want* to be friends."

Impatience flared inside him. Christ, couldn't they just get this over with? Like ripping off a fucking Band-Aid, why prolong the agony? "Then what the fuck do you mean?"

"Don't rush me! This is hard!"

His heart softened at her anguished tone. "Take your time, Lex," he muttered. "Got all day." Then he muttered under his breath, "To get my heart kicked in."

Lexi frowned and blinked rapidly. "I meant, my feelings have changed, because…I'm in love with you."

Every nerve in his body went on alert, but he didn't move. Still kept his face neutral. What. The. Fuck? In love with him? Had he heard that right?

"I know you're seeing someone else," she said quietly. "And if that's serious, I don't want to interfere."

"I saw her once." Serious? About Heather? Jesus.

"Okay." She licked her lips, her pulse fluttering rapidly

in her throat. "But still, I don't want to—"

"Is that what this is about?" he barked. "You saw me with Heather and now you think you're in love with me?"

"Um. No…well, not exactly." Her eyes got shiny like she was going to cry.

"Then what exactly?" He was pushing it. He knew he was. But he had to know. Was this for real? Because he didn't think he could handle having his heart stomped on one more time.

She sighed but kept her chin lifted. "I was jealous when I saw you with her," she said quietly. "I admit it. At first, I didn't realize what was wrong with me. I didn't like seeing you with her, and I couldn't figure out why it bugged me that much. It took the rest of the weekend thinking about it, talking about it, to figure out why. It's because I love you."

He watched her talk, taking in her earnest expression, the uncertainty flickering in her eyes, her fingers twisting together. Fuck, fuck, fuck. Was this really happening?

"I—" She paused. "I want you to know that I wasn't using you."

He frowned.

"Vanda accused me of using you. As my stand-in boyfriend. And yes, I sort of did, but if you ever felt used or taken advantage of, I want t-to apologize. I th-thought we had fun together. I never intended to use you or make you feel bad, and if you did, I am so, so sorry."

Her voice shook a little. She paused for a breath.

"I thought I didn't want a relationship," she continued, voice still low. "I was too busy for guys who were annoyed by my career. I want time for me. For my friends. Vanda accused me of being selfish, too, but now I think it wasn't just me being selfish—"

"Vanda's had a lot to say to you lately," he muttered.

"Um. Yeah. But she was only trying to help. And she did." She gave an earnest little nod. "She just wanted me to see what I was really doing."

"Which is?"

"It was just that I hadn't met the right guy. Papa helped me realize that, too. Because with most guys it seemed like a lot of work, being with them. But...it never was with you. Papa also made me realize that...maybe I wasn't completely open to a relationship. Because I was afraid."

She looked down at her hands. "Some men I've gone out with can't deal with my dads," she continued in a low voice. "I had no time for anyone like that, but sometimes...it hurt. If I met someone I thought I could care about and that was how they felt...maybe all along I've just been protecting my heart." She sucked in another breath. "Anyway, I wanted to apologize and..." She rose to her feet and started edging to the door. "I'm sorry." She gave him an almost gruesome smile. "And I-I wish it could have been otherwise, but I'm glad we were friends, Mac. I'll let you, um, get back to whatever...you were doing."

She barreled toward the door, bashed into an armchair, bounced off it, stumbled, righted herself, and continued her trajectory to the exit.

"Jesus," he muttered. He had to save her from herself. Plus, he couldn't let her go.

As her hand closed around the doorknob, he caught her, arms sliding around her middle, hauling her back against him. "Stop," he said. "Lexi. Fuck."

She went stiff in his arms. "Mac. Let me go."

"Fuck no." He pressed his face to her hair, and his arms secured her even more. "I'm not letting you go. Not ever."

She took a big shuddering breath.

He turned her in his arms to face his chest, and she stared for two seconds at his Dr. Who T-shirt that said "Keep calm and don't blink." Then he cupped the back of her head in one hand and pressed her face to his chest. "You sure, Lexi?" he murmured. "Are you really sure?"

"Sure about what? Sure that I love you?"

"Yeah. Because, fuck me, if this is just some crazy whim because you were jealous seeing me with Heather—"

"No!" She jerked her head back to look at him. Their eyes met in a blaze of heat, hers wide and honest. "No! I *was* jealous, but I've spent all weekend thinking about this and… and…I've loved you for a long time. I was just too stupid to realize it."

Joy exploded in him, his heart banging against his ribs. "Not stupid." He crushed her to him. Christ, he was shaking. "Fuck, not stupid. Thank fuck. Thank fuck." He rocked her a little in his arms.

"So…um… does this mean…"

"Yeah. Fuck yeah. I love you, too, Lexi." His language was awful, but he was so worked up it just poured out.

"Oh god." She threw her arms around his neck and tried to climb his body to get to his mouth. "Oh god, Mac."

Their mouths met, hard, desperate, needy. They kissed fiercely, feverishly. One of his hands still in her hair, the other on her ass, he held her anchored against him. When finally they broke apart and stared at each other, they were both panting for air.

"Seriously?" he asked again, needing to be reassured

that this was really happening.

She touched her fingers to his eyebrow, smoothed over it, then his forehead and into his hair. "Seriously."

His eyes closed. "I've loved you for fucking ever, Lex." His voice came out gruff.

"Really?"

"Really." He leaned his forehead against hers. "Christ."

"I'm so relieved," she choked out. "I love you, Mac."

"Love you, too, baby." His mouth met hers again, this time slower and sweeter. "Let me show you."

"Oh…yes."

He swung her up into his arms. She grabbed on. "Mac!"

He grinned. "You're not getting away."

• • •

He strode down the hall to his bedroom. The last time she'd been there he'd been sick. Now, he was apparently very healthy and fit. He carried her to his bed, dropped her there, and covered her body with his.

She'd been so scared. She'd confessed her love for him, and instead of grabbing her and kissing her and telling her he loved her, too, he'd shouted at her. Searching for some graceful way to get out of there, to make her exit and keep her dignity, she'd instead careened across the room, crashing into furniture and nearly landing on her ass. That chair was going to leave a bruise. Ah, well. The relief at knowing he loved her erased the pain of a little bruise. Emotion swelled up inside her, huge and hot.

Settling between her legs, his elbows planted into the bed, he framed her face with his hands and gazed into her eyes for a long moment. Her hands clutched his back as they stared at each other with love and longing and anticipation.

He bent his head to gently suck her top lip, then her bottom lip, then kissed her nose and eyelids. "Lex."

"Yes. Yes, Mac. Kiss me." She gripped his big shoulders and held on tight. She was never letting him go.

They kissed again and again. He buried his hands in her hair, holding her head. His lips were firm and sure on hers, opening her to him. He drew her bottom lip between his and sucked, then stroked his tongue over it. Liquid heat pooled between her thighs, and she pushed up against his hard body, seeking more pressure where she needed it. She ached low inside, a deep ravenous ache that had her hips rolling against his.

Her hands slid everywhere she could reach—his arms, his shoulders, his back. She cupped his firm ass through his jeans, pulling him harder against her aching core. His fingers in her hair had sensation cascading down her spine.

"Love you, Lex." He nuzzled the side of her neck, then closed his lips over her earlobe, his breath tickling her. She gave a full-bodied shiver. "So damn much."

Her heart was swelling up huge in her chest, relief and love expanding inside her. God, she loved him. She loved him. Her world felt suddenly different. Open. Expanding. Bright and beautiful. "I love you, too."

She planted a foot into the mattress and rolled him so she was on top, kissing him again, everywhere—his throat, his neck, his strong jaw. She breathed in his scent. "You smell good." She touched her tongue to his skin. "And taste good, too."

A groan rumbled in his chest. His hand slipped inside

her yoga pants to squeeze her ass.

His groan made her inner muscles clench. She couldn't get enough of him, the taste of him in her mouth, the feel of him against her. She found his skin beneath the T-shirt, pressed her hips into his, feeling his erection behind the fly of his jeans. He moaned again as she did that, and again when she slipped a hand between them to his groin, covering his hard cock.

"Mac." His name was a sigh on her lips.

"Right here, baby. Right here with you."

Thank god. Thank god he was.

He rolled her, trapping her under him once more.

"That feels good." Her voice came out husky. Her hands slid into his hair, savoring the thick, silky feel of it. "I love how heavy you are on me."

"Don't wanna hurt you."

"Mmm. You're not." She pulled his mouth down to hers.

He cupped her face, fingers sliding beneath her ears, one thumb teasing the corner of her mouth, then tugging her lower lip down, opening her for him. He angled his head and dipped to kiss her, his tongue sweeping into her mouth.

He eased to the side and slipped his hand under her tank top to find her breast, thumbing her nipple. A hard shiver worked over her body. Her breasts swelled and ached for his touch. He took his time, teasing her, making her crazed with need, finally cupping one breast and gently squeezing.

She groaned and nipped at his bottom lip. He smiled against her mouth, his nose pressed alongside her. She opened her eyes to meet his. The beauty and love and worship she saw there melted her, and she could only gaze helplessly back at him. "I love you, Mac."

The stretchy yoga clothes came off without difficulty. She didn't even have a bra under the snug tank top, and was soon wearing only her black thong panties. "I was doing yoga," she informed him breathlessly.

His lips twitched. "Glad to hear it."

She smiled, too. "You *should* be glad. I'm very flexible."

"Is that right?" He went to his knees, reached behind him to grab a fistful of his T-shirt, then yanked it off forward over his head. She studied him in his jeans, low on lean hips, abs rippling as he moved. She took in his handsome, square-jawed face shadowed with stubble, his beautiful sculpted mouth that had earlier been so grim. With masculine grace, he flicked open the button of his jeans, undid his fly, and shoved them down his hips.

Her mouth fell open at seeing his cock. "Wow…I never knew you were such a rebel."

He gave a low chuckle and got rid of the jeans. "I was naked when the doorman called up." He reached into the drawer of the bedside table and pulled out a condom.

"Shut up."

"No lie."

She watched his hands as he rolled on the condom, heat building inside her. "What were you doing?"

"You don't wanna know."

"Maybe I do."

He returned to the bed and kissed her mouth. "Use your imagination."

"Does it involve porn?"

He choked on another laugh. "Not this time. I was thinking about you."

"Mmm." Her heart squeezed at hearing that.

Now naked, he moved over her. Heat sizzled down her spine and centered low inside her, intensifying as he shifted and kissed his way down to her breasts. "I believe you owe me a blow job," he murmured as he settled between her thighs.

She parted them to accommodate him, loving how perfectly he fit. She throbbed there, needing more of him, but her eyes widened at his words.

"I do," she whispered breathlessly. She pushed excitedly at his shoulder. "Let me—"

"No." His one word was decisive. "Not this time."

"But—"

"What was that about anyway?" He nuzzled her hair, kissed her jaw.

"Oh." It was hard to remember, with his heat and weight pushing her down, their naked bodies pressed together. "I thought maybe you didn't want to be friends with benefits because the sex was no good for you."

He made a choking noise.

"I wanted to make it better...do something for you..." Her words trailed away as his tongue dragged up the side of her neck.

He snorted. "If the sex had been any better, I'd have been unconscious. Jesus, Lexi."

"So it was good?" She didn't like to seem insecure, but she wanted to hear it.

"It was fucking amazing."

"Oh." She sighed. He licked her throat, then sucked gently, reaching for his cock to guide it inside her. "That's what I thought, too. So amazing."

He pushed inside her, filling her lusciously, perfectly, a

sweet pressure connecting them so intimately it made her shiver. She couldn't look away. She moved with him, welcoming him inside her and squeezing, holding on to him with her arms and legs and her whole body, showing him how she felt.

"Thank you," she whispered.

"For what?" He rocked, his hips powering, the friction of his hard cock within her exquisite.

"For loving me."

He closed his eyes. "Don't thank me." He groaned. "Don't thank me for loving you. Christ, I can't fucking help it. And… it's my honor."

Her heart stuttered and her lips parted, gazing up at him. "Holy crap," she whispered. "I'm the luckiest girl in the world."

"And don't you forget it." His eyes drifted closed on another long, delicious slide into her body.

She smiled, even as sensation built beautifully in her core.

"I never felt used, Lex," he muttered. "Never. I knew you liked being with me."

"I did. I do. So much." She was close, the sensation of him sliding along sensitized nerve endings, pushing deep and hitting *that* spot, shot her up to the stars at a dizzying speed. Heat built and twisted, rising higher and higher, her body rising with it. She went so high it almost hurt, a sharp point of ecstasy, and then it burst. Ripples of exquisite pleasure flowed from her center, intense and yet such a sweet relief she could have cried from it. Stunning. Beautiful. Powerful. "I love you, Mac." She tightened her grip on him, sweet pleasure coursing in her veins, spreading through her body.

He fell over her, shoved his face into the side of her

neck, thrust into her once, twice, then went taut and still, a long groan escaping him. "Love. You. Too."

"You were making me nuts," he mumbled, long moments later, when they were tangled up together beneath the sheet. She sighed with pleasure, loving the scrape of his beard stubble against her jaw, the slow thud of his heart against her chest, the smell of him.

"All the times we were together, I kept thinking it was going to happen, it was happening. I was dying for you, Lex. Dying."

"Oh, god." His words thrilled her to her core, but also made her ache with regret for lost time and how she must have hurt him. She couldn't speak, her throat clogged with tears and emotion. If only she'd figured things out sooner. She hated that he'd been hurting because of her and could still hardly believe he loved her, too.

"Then we slept together. I was sure that meant your feelings had changed. I was sure that was it. But it wasn't. It fucking killed me."

"I'm sorry. I'm so sorry." She touched his face with her fingers, then kissed the corner of his mouth.

"You kept insisting we were just friends. That day you brought me home, when I was sick, I felt like such a loser. On top of being humiliated when I showed up at your place for dinner with flowers, thinking we were finally more than friends… I couldn't do it anymore. I figured I had to give up hoping you were ever going to love me. Stop torturing myself by spending time with you. That was why I went out with Heather."

She scowled. But she couldn't blame him. She'd been such an idiot.

"You were giving up on us?" she asked softly, chest aching.

"Yeah. Maybe. I don't know. I don't know if I ever could, but after that day I was determined I was done with hoping. A guy can only take so much torture."

She nodded against his shoulder. "I know. I'm sorry. I know it's not the same, but all weekend I was miserable. Once I realized that I loved you and I'd screwed it all up and it was probably too late...I was so frackin' mad at my-self. I could not *believe* how I'd messed up. But Papa and Vanda were both telling me I should tell you how I felt. They seemed to think you felt the same." She smiled at him and traced her index finger over his bottom lip.

He winced. "You told your dads about us?"

Her smile deepened. "Only Papa. Dad doesn't want to hear about my love life. But Papa is good with it. I mean, I didn't go into detail, but I told him how confused I was." She paused. "He said he thought you were crazy about me."

"I *am* crazy about you," he growled.

Now she grinned. "Thank god. I was terrified. I couldn't give up hope that Papa was right and maybe there was a chance you felt the same, but oh my god, I was scared. The idea that you would reject me because you were with an-other girl...holy snap, that just shredded me."

"Never." He turned to press his lips to her temple. "Never gonna happen. Not now."

"I never realized how terrifying it was to love someone." She closed her eyes at the touch of his lips to her forehead. "I thought I was too busy for a relationship. I thought it was easy just being friends with you." A thought occurred to her, and she went still. "Maybe I actually *did* realize how scary it was, and that's why I was in denial about my feelings for you."

"In denial. Yeah."

She tipped her chin up to smile into his eyes. "I'd rather think I was in denial than stupid."

He smiled back at her and slid his hand over her jaw, around the side of her neck, his thumb brushing her cheek in front of her ear. "Sometimes we deny the truth until we're ready to accept it."

Her belly fluttered at his words, and she stared at him, mesmerized, humbled by his forgiveness and understanding.

"I'm glad you were ready, Lex."

"Me, too." She closed her fingers around his wrist to hold his hand on her neck. "Oh, me, too."

About the Author

Kelly Jamieson is a best-selling author of over thirty-five romance novels and novellas. Her writing has been described as "emotionally complex," "sweet and satisfying," and "blisteringly sexy." She likes coffee (black), wine (mostly white), shoes (high), and watching hockey! She loves hearing from readers, so please visit her website at http://www.kellyjamieson.com, sign up for her newsletter, or contact her at info@kellyjamieson.com.

www.ingramcontent.com/pod-product-compliance
Lightning Source LLC
Chambersburg PA
CBHW070557180626
46817CB00005B/1876